The Misconceptions That Misleads Us

By

Fareed Ray

ISBN-978-1-7361325-1-7

We Help You Self-Publish Your Book
Crystell Publications
PO BOX 8044 / Edmond – OK 73083
www.crystellpublications.com
(405) 414-3991

Printed in the USA

THE MISCONCEPTIONS THAT MISLEADS US

Allah distinguished man with the gift of "mind" giving him reference for; responsibility, accountability, reward and punishment!

DEDICATION

I dedicate this book to my lil' brother, Tariq Wesley Ray (RIP). I love you and I apologize for not being a better big brother and role model. The Feds gave me a lot of time to sit, think, and reflect. I now realize we were deceived big time. I don't want to be a player no more. I got daughters! I don't want to be a gangster or a thug. I lost you! Once you lose your life you can't change it! So, why not change it before you lose it?

ACKNOWLEDGEMENTS

I would first like to acknowledge the creator of the heavens and the earth. It's only through Allah's (God's) grace and mercy that I was able to see this vision and know my purpose in life.

Next, I'd like to acknowledge and thank my children. Everything bad about my life, you made right. I love you all: Tyear, Fareed Jr., Quadir, Tyson, Auanise, Laicie, Journee, Justice, and An-Nisa.

I also gotta thank all the guys I did time with during those trying times when we were away from our families for long periods of time. We acted as a crutch for each other when we went through major losses (family etc.), and when we didn't have things; we were able to lean on each other. Much love for the entire Pennsylvania at FCI Schuylkill. I must thank you guys. My Harrisburg Boys! You couldn't have put me around a better group of young, thorough men. Big homie Gizz, Ang, Lid, Black Locc. Living on the unit with them for all them years always made me feel a little at home. The love and conversation with them was priceless.

Can't forget about T-Roy, my lil'-big bro', Whop. We came a long way from when you were 11 years old, running around the 'hood when I first met you. We laughed all the time saying who would have thought, back then, that we would end up in the Fed's together. Our lives are headed in better directions now. I'd go to the end of the earth with you and for you. Finish ya project and make it part of history.

My big-lil' cuz, P-Nut, how we never came to blows is beyond me. You used to joke and say you had to "stop yaself from punching me in the head" when I used to be sleep in the cell! (I know the truth is told through jokes.) You felt ya way and I felt mine because at different times we were both wrong. Still, forgiveness was made by us both. Waking up with 21 years to do, you was right there helping me keep my head in the game. Love is love; thank you, you grumpy-ass, old man!

Much love to D.C. My DC dudes showed me love. Gucci, you know I ain't forget about you and Bob. My guys from New York, much love to you as well. Especially my guy "EB" Ernest Hester. You're one of the main reasons I completed this book. You pushed me, bro. You went home and did everything you said you would and

i

sent my daughter money for her birthday. All these years of seeing dudes leave and never look back. But when its real, its real.

My guy "E", Erick Hicks from D.C. If you ever seen "For Life," the 50 Cent TV show you will know the guy that becomes the lawyer in jail and helps so many people give time back on appeals. He's that guy in the flesh, if not better. If you ever get a chance to meet this man, you'll see from the door how authentic and real he is — last of a dying breed. Thank you for everything, ya wisdom and ya favorite line to me, "Don't panic." I look forward to the day I can repay you for what you did for me.

Keith Cash, thanks Big Bro'. You had to be the most instrumental person for me during this journey. Talking for hours enabled me to see my visions clearly. Had it not been for you, I'd probably still be saying, "I'll finish tomorrow." My brother Beans, for you to be so young, you got an old soul and a good heart. Thank you for adding your story to the book.

I cannot forget my Baltimore guys, in all this love-giving. Brother Moe and of course, Gorrock, thank you for adding ya thoughts to the book.

To all my bros, I remember the brotherhood, the love, the feeling you get when we all come together to do good. Thank you to all the Imams: Ubaid, Sameed, Abdul-Salam, Quddus, Ala-meen. The last two conversations with Quddus and Ala-meen stuck with me. I'm grateful for Hadeeb, Donnie, Ibraheem, Betim Kaziu, SP, and Ryeese, Abdul Raheem (Dion) and my big bro', Wise. I cannot forget about you Mujah, you helped me through some hard days. What would I have done without our talks or you setting up shop in ya cell for me? (ha-ha!) Joemon Higdon, you know I got you, you big head joker. I'm running out of space. I'd be here all day writing every bro's name. I love all y'all for the sake of Allah!

I would like to give a special thanks to Tyrisha Roberson. After 23 years, you're still here in my life. A lot of my first important lessons come from you. I couldn't get things right. I still wanted to be a boy and not a man. I'm sorry about all I took you through, and I love you!

Another special thanks goes to my girlfriend forever, Rasheeta Wilson. Words cannot express how grateful I am to have you in my life, and I'm so glad you went on this journey with me. I could not have done this without your help, love and support. Your love has pushed me through at times when I did not have much to give. The visits, letters, phone calls and even all the arguments have shaped us and prepared us for the good, the bad, and the ugly. This logo, this business, this success is yours more than mine. You invested in me, gave what you didn't have, and never asked for anything in return. You just wanted to see me win, and for that I love you. I appreciate your sacrifice, and I will not let you down.

Now, without further ado, I speak to the best woman I know, my mother, Arlean. You never gave up on me, and I love you. How precious and sweet you are. When I was first convicted, you said, "I'm getting a loan to get you a lawyer, because of the way you took care of your kids. She didn't say she was proud of me, maybe that is what fathers are supposed to do. But, during my reflections, it made me think of the last time she said she was proud of me, and I couldn't remember the last time. but that was because for years, I've done everything contrary to what she tried to teach me. Yet, since then, I made a vow to make my mother proud. That has been the best achievement I've ever accomplished. Making you smile and hoping I've made you proud of me. Your children are great, your father is great timer your grandparents are great, but, there's no one more precious than your mother. Thank you I love you, Mom.

I give lots of love to two of the best grandmas ever: Elista Waters (Tiny) and Dorothy Reeves-McClure (RIP). To my three grandpops: Oscar L. Reeves (RIP), Warren Ray (RIP), and Les Waters (RIP), and to Quandra and Wink — thank y'all. To my father Warren Ray, love you, Dad. To all my children's mothers, thank y'all Aleecia Greene, Kisha Venable (RIP), Betty English, and Annet Rivera for the gifts you gave me. I also must thank these other mothers: Reba Harris (RIP), Aunt Deb, Aunt Val, Alveese Banks, Ms. Michelle, and my other mother, Leslie.

Synopsis

The Misconceptions that Mislead Us

This book includes real-life situations, scenarios, and experiences of real people who were misled and misguided by the very same misconceptions that are learned by millions of young boys and girls, growing up in our urban communities.

"If you don't learn the correct way to love, be committed, work hard, have relations, parent, and other essential correct ways of living, then you're definitely subject to learn the wrong way," says Fareed Ray.

This book taps into the thoughts of young adolescents' minds as they are learning how to process their ways, thoughts, and behaviors, as well as what causes us to adopt wrong behaviors.

The book also visits some solution ideas for how we can correct and recondition some of the errors in our thinking. It offers examples of how we can teach our youth to be comfortable enough to come to us and ask for help when they need it. These experiences will help us avoid a lot of the unnecessary downfalls within our communities and families, especially if we pay attention to who's teaching our youth and what they are being taught. Ask yourself, "Could I have been misled by any or all these misconceptions? Could I have been deceived?"
If you have, what can we do to save the next generation?

Let's hit the reset button! It has to stop and restart somewhere. Why not correct it for you and yours now, and those who will come? If you truly love them, this book will help to initiate a fresh start.

Introduction

I was forced to change my way of thinking and the way I see things. I always made comments like "they" boxed me in, meaning how they put me in jail. Truth be told, I boxed myself in. Due to my actions and misconceptions, I was forced to spend 21 years in jail. That meant I didn't see any of my children graduate. Hell No! I don't accept that, I reject that! I love each one of them crumb snatchers, and I got to be there for them because I love them, right? What about when I did have the opportunity to be there for them? Did I even understand what being a father meant? I said I love them, but did I truly know what it meant to love them?

Not only was I forced to change my way of thinking and seeing things, I was forced to write this book so that I can own my truths – shed some light on not just the error of my ways and thinking, but also to acknowledge that it's not just me who thought and saw things this way. Now, what can we do to save and help each other avoid this? We can question what was taught to us.

I chose my title for the book because a lot of people have these same thoughts and theories. More times than not, we first encounter these misconceptions, thoughts, and theories in youth. Whether that be from firsthand experiences or the experiences of others, that led us to believe these things to be true. Throughout this book, you will come across more than one misconception that you may have believed to be true. My wish and desire are for you to open your mind a little, reevaluate your thoughts, and look at things from another perspective. I'm doing this all to help recondition our minds and better educate ourselves and, more importantly, today's youth.

My words are from personal experience. I, Fareed Ray, was led by a lot of these misconceptions, which misled me in life. I was not educated on certain beliefs, which influenced a lot of my behavior. Now at 39 years of age, seeing my own children being misled and not properly educated about the basic aspects of living a right life, I wish to help youth stop being blinded and deceived, so that we can break this vicious cycle that leads so many to jail and death, especially when we don't value the little things and the most important things in life. Take a journey with me as I share my experiences and the experiences of others, that may challenge or change how we see and do things....

IN THE UNITED STATES DISTRICT COURT
FOR THE MIDDLE DISTRICT OF PENNSYLVANIA
HARRISBURG DIVISION

UNITED STATES OF AMERICA,	)CASE NO.
Plaintiff	)1:12-CR-0058-02
Vs.	)
FAREED RAY,	)
Defendant	)

Another day I'll never forget. The day the Indictment was handed down. You never forget the feeling of walls being closed in on you.

wheCase: 15-1880 Document: 003112584436 Page: 7 Date Filed: 04/05/2017

STATEMENT OF THE CASE

On February 2, 2012, local law enforcement initiated an investigation of and arrested Fareed Ray, a/k/a "Diego," the defendant. Police received permission to search the car he was in and found cocaine and other evidence of drug trafficking. At the police station, police searched the defendant more thoroughly and recovered more cocaine hidden on the defendant. The United States Drug Enforcement Administration adopted the case, and it was indicted shortly thereafter.

The defendant tried to suppress the evidence found during the search of the car and the search of his person, but the district court denied the motion. The defendant now appeals the ruling, and he seeks to vacate his convictions for drug trafficking and firearms offenses and vacate his 248-month sentence.

That 248-month sentence could have been 540 months (45 years) because I lost every count (charge) at trial. However, because nobody else got more than 12 years on the case they couldn't give me that much time because it would have been considered an unwarranted disparity.

IRVIN KITTRELL III, The Patriot-News

A man sought on drug charges was captured after wrecking a minivan at Seventh and Maclay streets in Harrisburg on Friday, police said.

Drug suspect caught

CHAPTER 1

Being a Gangster or Thug Is Cool

The concept of being a gangster or thug is cool. There is nothing cool about waking up in jail knowing that you're NEVER going home again. Knowing that you'll never be able to be with a woman again. Knowing that you'll never see your children graduate. You'll never be able to just be there when your children need you Your mother, sister, or brother need you. No wedding and even no funeral to see your loved ones off.

I begin with this subject because this is the reality of so many people. It also affects families, mothers, and children. I am surrounded by countless men that may very well NEVER be able to make it out, unless the courts grant them relief from some of the unjust laws made years ago to target minorities. As much as a man in this situation may try to hide or disguise his true feelings, you cannot hide how you really feel when, as Paolo Coelho's well-known statement goes: "the eyes are the mirror of the soul."

Some will try to trick you, but they are only trying to convince themselves when they make statements such as "it is what it is," or "it ain't about nothing." It is about something. It is about your life and you only get one. So, unless you can live, then die, and come back to live again, you should put more stock into this one life you are given!

Still, this is the image that has been placed on being a gangster or thug. You know it because the gangster has always been perceived, as well as portrayed as cool and tough. Even the women want themselves a bad boy or a gangster. You can go far back, to children playing cops and robbers (in my generation). I doubt the kids play that in this day and age when they have Grand Theft Auto and games like it to enchant them. This is just an example. Everyone wanted to be the robber. Nobody jumped at being the cop. We wanted to be chased to see if we could elude capture. Why? Because early on our impressionable minds were conditioned. Being the bad guy has always been attractive to so many.

The gangster got the money, power, respect, and the girls. "Sign me up, I can handle it," is what misguided, uneducated adolescents say every day! But can you really handle it? It is already attractive. Plus, it's a shortcut to success and quick monetary gain because there is very little requirement that comes with being a thug. As long as you're tough, can be cold-hearted, cutthroat, a villain, and a crook, then you're starting off with a master's degree from the College of Hard Knocks.

To be this gangster or thug, you gotta love everything that comes with the lifestyle, the good and the bad of it. You love the area and neighborhood; you love those inside your circle, gang, or organization because it's looked upon as a brotherhood. Let me tell you about this so-called brotherhood. Let me tell you about all the things you don't see coming into this thing of "ours", mimicking the mafia's slang. Because truth be told, that's where we get it from or saw it first. We saw a gangster or thug being cool and attractive. So, we wanted to imitate what we saw, especially if it was a means to a better life. That's why most "wannabe" thugs tell themselves they want to or should be a gangster. They're the ones that already have a rough life and feel like nothing was ever given to them, so they are "ready to take it." They don't have much or may not have anyone really to be there for them. Fathers missing in action (jail, dead, or on drugs) and moms having to work all day every day to make ends meet. It's easier for them to turn to the streets, since, "What do I have to lose?"

Before you take that leap, you really need to know everything about this life and what it brings. You need to know that a lot of times, people are loyal and love you when it's convenient and beneficial for *them*. You also need to know that more people than you think have a breaking point! So, when someone says, "Death before dishonor," does he or she really mean it?

Don't believe the hype every time! Does it just sound good when someone says it — or when they may even get it tattooed on their body. I mean because, as black men, we gotta look the part and sound like the part. Ride or Die! But then ask yourself, how many are truly down to die for you? Who wants to die, period, let alone, die for you! That must be one of the most over-exaggerated statements I ever heard.

Personally, I have heard so-called gangsters say, "I ain't doing life in jail for nobody," or "I ain't doing life in jail for something I didn't do." But this is what you signed up for, right? So, even if you didn't agree with what happened, you are "committed" to the good *and the bad* that comes with it. Yet, these words don't always ring true. You come to learn and find out that, most times, people are more loyal when it's convenient. This is what you don't see in the beginning. You don't see all the true colors until you (or they) are put in a tough spot. So, when they (or you) scream, "Death before dishonor," is it really? Will they die for you or do life for you? It is easy to say if you have never met a breaking point. You know, a point of no return.

Let's say you're living this gangster life, and someone kidnaps you. He threatens to kill you, possibly your child, and maybe your mother if you don't give him what he wants! The kidnapper asks for your friend's address and says to call him to meet you. Will you let your mother or child die? Then, what about getting locked up, facing life in jail but "they" give you the opportunity to tell on a friend in order to save yourself from doing life? These are some of what I call breaking points. So many that have faced these types of situations and breaking points have most certainly broke. Be real with yourself if your so-called friend was the one that set you up to get robbed in the process. You survive, but your child loses her life, or your mother or wife does. Was it worth it then?

In fact, so many have faced way less severe circumstances and have broken. That *Death before Dishonor* slogan went right out the window! A new quote was put into place, "The number one role of man is self-preservation." Even though this didn't describe what they were doing, they made it fit in order to justify what they were doing. When it comes down to you and him, just ask yourself, "How many really down to die for you, or willing to do life for you?"

Now that I touched on that, let me take you down a more sensitive road. A very real road. A road that is so familiar to so many. You gotta be able to recognize that the streets don't love nobody. The streets do, in some cases, lead to some success, but numbers don't lie. More people lose than actually win.

My story is just like so many other stories. A story of pain, failure, deception, and loss. These words best describe my experience trying to be a gangster or thug. Hearing my story or parts of my story will, hopefully, save someone's life or maybe even several people's lives. Everybody should feel like this, "I know my story gets better because I know the author. Keep reading, it's a comeback story." Fab's Cold Summer lyrics! What I got from that is: (1) Know yourself but know the most-high first; after the creator, we are in control of our own destiny because we have free will to go left or right; and (2) Know that you can make lemonade from lemons.

So, I took every bad thing that happened to me and I began to use it to motivate me and push me to be better on all cylinders. I don't know how sincere it was in the beginning. All I did know was that I needed to try something different, and I wanted to make a few people proud of me, like my mom, my lady, and my children, because that is all I had left once the smoke cleared.

The first thing I did allowed me to see the comeback story come alive. I began going to school to be a certified paralegal. Why this was so monumental is because I got indicted by the feds in 2012. Some bogus charges if you ask me, but I was doing some things that I shouldn't have. We all know everything comes with a price, so I had to pay the price of my actions and decisions. Even though I know these charges were bullshit, I was up against one of the most powerful entities in the world. The United States of America's Federal Government. How do you go into a fight knowing that you're going to lose? I guess, it's just hoping you don't lose on every charge and there can be some light at the end of the tunnel, after the outcome. I was facing life in jail, well actually, forty-five years to be exact. At thirty years old, forty-five years was considered life – especially when a black man's average life expectancy is about sixty-eight years old! Sitting in the county jail I am saying to myself: Unless the creator of the worlds allows me to beat these charges or some of them, I could very well die in jail! At the time, I got a whole basketball team of children with two more on the way. I am really like, "Damn! This is how it ends? This what being a gangster or thug leads to? My undoing like this though?" They didn't even really catch me red handed or nothing. It was just some people saying I did some things. But this is how the feds work and all they need is hearsay. Of course, the government offered to reduce the charges and time if I gave up my cousin and a dude, I thought was my brother. Nevertheless, from the door, I knew I would rather die in jail than tell! I mean, this is how it is supposed to go, right? Never tell. "Take the hit for your friend." (Words from the gangster movie, Good Fellas)

So, while you do your time, your gang or homies supposed to look out for you; set you out, make sure your kids are cool and your lady is good. Now, that is where mimicking the movies goes left because in real life, when you in jail, you on your own. More times than none, you in jail and your homie messing with your lady or baby moms. Yeah, this is the flipside to being a gangster or thug, the stuff you first don't see coming in. No way will they tell you, "Yeah, you my bro' but, if opportunity presents itself, I may betray you." Or "I didn't mean for it to happen; it kind of just happened." When you fall victim to one of these circumstances, or maybe all of them, you come to realize you were deceived, you were tricked, you were so naive. Where is the loyalty? What happen to *Death before Dishonor*? Well, in all actuality, you tricked yourself. You tried to convince yourself that you were smarter than so many others that fell victim before you did. You are not!

I said all that to say this: in my situation, I was stuck. I could not trust my lawyer, she lied to me and deceived me. To this day, I don't know why, but everything come to the light. That's another story, though. Being that I couldn't trust my attorney, I had to educate myself. They say if you want to hide something from a black man put it in a book. Real shit! Back in the days, people would hide their valuables in cut out pages of books on bookshelves because if their homes were broken into by black people, they'd never mess with the books. Sad part is that the truth is told through jokes because, even to this day, we will pick up a book last. We will trade war stories, talk about women and money as a way to pass time in jail. But I told myself that it is time to change that narrative. I had to learn about the law and find my way out. Then, did my fight for freedom become that much more intriguing as I learned and became a certified paralegal. It amazed me at how they been playing us for all these years because we didn't know no better. When you know better, you do better. Now, I've become not only a certified paralegal, but an author too.

While being a gangster or thug you can never fully be committed to a female you love or care about because you're already committed to and married to the streets. My daughters know and the youngest will know. I tell them, "Love a man like your dad was and you're sure to experience a lot of pain and suffering, as it will bring you down and be your undoing – the undoing of everything you work for."

That misconception right here hits so close to home! I definitely thought being a gangster or thug was cool. So did my little brother Tariq, may he rest in peace. His death hit me hard and still does because *I* could have made something else look cool and thorough. So many of our youth are dazzled by this lifestyle. This lifestyle that claims life as well as long sentences in jail or the graveyard. Is that part of it cool and thorough? Especially when you jump right in the game, gang, or street life and don't get nothing out of it. So many don't even win at all. Don't even accumulate any real money or even leave the 'hood at all. They end up dying within the first year of living life or they end up getting locked up and sentenced to a quarter century (twenty-five years). How much sense or cents does that make? If you gotta die, why not die for something that means something or something worth it – something like dying to protect your family or children.

Somewhere along the line you convinced yourself that you could win, you convinced yourself that you could walk away, once you got what you needed. I know I did. I used to tell my lady how I only need about six months and then I'm done. I remember her asking, "What if right before you get to the date, something happens, you get arrested or worse, lose your life?" I used to say nothing's gonna happen. But I was wrong; she was right. I got sentenced to 248 months (twenty years and eight months).

If you think it cannot happen to you, don't be fooled. When you're sitting in jail with more years to do in jail than you even lived yet and your homies won't even send you a dime, remember this. One of the homies always wanted what you had, so his intentions were to get with your baby mother, and he succeeded too. Now he's raising your kid, showing him everything not to do. This one takes the cake! Other dudes catch a similar break as you, but they end up "cooperating" and they do little or no time before they're back out there. To add insult to injury, they back getting money, yet they got on the stand and everybody knows, but it don't even matter. If this happens to you, you gonna feel so stupid and deceived. Yet, you deceived yourself!

When is or when was enough really enough? Will it ever be enough? This is what you have to ask yourself. Take a good look in the mirror. No one on this earth should know you better than you know yourself! This is where you have to be honest with yourself. If me being a gangster or thug leads to my early death, how would I feel knowing all the hurt, pain and anguish my mother will have to endure burying her son? Parents want their kids to bury them and not have to bury their kids. How would it feel to know my daughters will never have their father there to protect them in this sometimes mean, cruel world?

My sons won't have a man to teach them how to be a good man and guide their decisions in life. After thinking about these questions and scenarios, if you feel nothing at the possibility or you don't at least say, "Damn!" or even say "I didn't look at it from that perspective," then something may be wrong with your mind and heart, if not both! Early death is a real possibility living the gangster life. I most definitely understand that we sometimes don't even look that far ahead because we just be living in the moment. It's more to just living in the moment. It's more to life than just you. If you cannot understand that, then you got the concept of life and living all the way fucked up. Excuse my language, but when you talk to the people, you have to speak in a tone and language they understand. The selfish, self-centered, and ignorant person may not even want to understand. Doesn't matter. Now is the time for us to understand. It's the time for us to save ourselves, time for us to save our families, time for us to stop being blind. Take the blindfold off so you can see clear. You can see you're about to walk over a cliff. See that you're driving head on into oncoming traffic!

For me personally, I knew enough was enough when my daughter used to come up on the visits and began to always ask me "When are you getting out of here, Daddy? Are you gonna be home by my birthday? It seems like you been in here forever!" She had to be about nine years old at the time, and I had been in jail since she was three and a half years old. I had been away from her for more years than she been alive, that's why it seemed like forever to her. All those years, I guess you can say I most certainly seen myself as a thug or gangster. I been thugging in these streets since I was twelve years old, before I even hit puberty. Breaking the law, being a follower. I really had no fear, but at that moment, there was no way I could tell her I'm not scheduled to come home until after she graduates from high school. I just didn't have the heart or courage to tell her that because I feared how she would take my truth. I didn't want to lie to her, so I curbed her question by asking her a question, "Do you believe in Allah or God?" She said "Yes" so I said, "If you pray hard for Daddy, maybe Allah/God will answer your prayers and bring Dad home sooner."

When I got sentenced to twenty plus years it hurt of course, but it didn't crush me. When you live the way I lived, and think the way I thought, only two ways can stop you. Death is one and getting crushed is the second. At that visit, I was crushed. I made up my mind, right then and there, *it's over for me. I have to "really" love my children more and do it the correct way a father is supposed to love, sacrifice, and support his children. I cannot take the type of pain that comes from a child's disappointment in his father, his hero*!

Sometimes you have to be able to learn from someone else's mistakes! They say a wise man learns from someone else's mistakes, and a fool learns from his own! I was a fool! You don't have to be. Learn from my mistakes and be the wise man! If you're sitting in a juvenile facility, placement or even jail, before you write these words off, I want you to think about one thing. Think about waking up in jail, knowing that you're NEVER going home again. It's a different type of wake up. In fact, some days you will dread waking up. Not because you want to die, but because you just wish you could stay in your dream a little longer, because you know that's the closest you get to being free. "You're greater than you think you are, and you're more than you're trying to be." - Brother Moe - (Baltimore Legend)

CHAPTER 2

Fatherhood

The average boy and most men are confused about fatherhood. He does not even understand what a father is supposed to be. This is a major problem because if we don't know what a father really is, how will we even be able to teach fatherhood? The key component in fatherhood is knowledge and understanding of what a good father is, then putting it into practice.

Being a good father doesn't just entail taking your children to the mall and getting them whatever they want. This is a very common misconception dealing with fatherhood and one I have come to realize very late in my life. All this time I was telling myself I was a good father or at least a decent father, but my children's mother gave it to me the realest. She said, "You're a good part-time father." I was used to just brushing her comments off because she has one of the slickest mouths ever. I charged it as her being slick until I was sitting in jail for a long period of time, and I had time to replay all of my actions and conversations I had. I then began to truly examine and judge myself as a father. That's when I realized she was right! I was good when I was there on the job but, due to the streets, jail, and my desires, I was only there part time. I cheated my children outta the life they were supposed to have with me, their father.

The importance of fatherhood! We didn't see it, and we don't fully understand it. This is part of the reason why we fall short in fatherhood. This is why we get caught up in the misconception of thinking what we can do to contribute is enough. Well, I'm here to tell you, it's mostly certainly not enough. What you think? Because you do buy things for you children and you see so many other men not doing anything that this makes you special of a good father? Absolutely NOT!!! This just means the bar has been set so low for us men to follow – especially us black men. That bars got to be at an all-time low for us being productive fathers too, for our children. Look at the fact that blacks account for 37% of the U.S. population yet we represent 67% of the prison population. Black men are nearly six times as likely to be incarcerated as everyone else. Do you know what factors into these numbers? It's the percentage of fatherless households we have among black families. I get it, every marriage or relationship won't last, but the fatherless households often mean no father presence in the children's life at all. So that's NO love, NO knowledge, NO direction or guidance from the man that brought them into this world. If children don't learn the right way, their bound to learn the wrong way! So, when a father sticks his chest out and says, "I take care of my kids," in the words of comedian Steve Harvey, "That's what you're supposed to do! What you want, a cookie?"

Yes, this is what you're supposed to do. But being a father is so much more than that.

A father is supposed to be the first man his daughter falls in love with. How important is this? Because from that love she understands what and how a man is supposed to make her heart feel, safe, secure, protected, and loved!

Too many times our daughters never receive that love from their fathers. They never know what real love is supposed to feel like. They are the ones that have what they call "daddy issues", always searching for the love they were deprived of and trying to fill that void. In their pursuit of trying to fill that void of finding that love they deserve, too many times they find the wrong type of love. They find lots of things that are disguised as love. By the time they realize it wasn't love, most times they've already lost so much. They lost time, money, property and even sometimes, they lost their way and themselves!

It's a part of ya fatherhood to see to it that you give your child a chance. Equip your child with the tools he or she will need to be successful and survive. This is your responsibility; this is your duty. When using words, we need to know the meaning of the word to say, this is what I am, or this is what I am not. Take the word father. Just because you have a child doesn't make you a father. A father is a male parent indeed, but a father treats, teaches, and takes care of his child. The three T's. When ya children are sick, you treat them and their sickness. When they don't know things, you teach them, and you overall take care of all their needs.

More times than none we may do one of these tasks and think we are good fathers. No. A good father takes care of all three tasks. When our child is sick, it's easy to get caught up in thinking, *oh that's the mother's job* or *she got it.* That's starting off with a misconception right there. It's both parents' job still, men will excuse themselves from particular duties because they perceive it to be "the woman's job". Have we not heard the Nigerian Igbo tribal saying, "It takes a village to raise a child"? That's exactly what it means! Besides, after God, the father is the originator in the process of a child coming. I say this because the seed comes from man. Before the baby can develop in the woman, it first takes the man to give his seed. Does man not know how important his role is in the child coming into this world? But aside from giving the seed, the truth of the matter is that we really don't know how to be a father. We don't see it enough, the correct way to be a father. Still, whether we see it enough or not, we feel it! You feel the love for your child the first time you see him or her. The first time you hold your baby in your arms. The love you have for them is supposed to enable you to be the best father you can be.

What about the misconception of thinking that because you and the child's mother are on bad terms or don't get along, it's okay to let the child suffer? A lot of boys think this is cool or okay, but it's not. I say boys because men don't move like that. How many times have we heard someone say, "I'm not doing nothing for that kid because their mom is this or that [or "...because she took me to child support court]!" That shit will roll off a person's tongue so easily too, without even thinking about what they were saying. What you should have done when you heard someone say that was to tell him how wrong he was for saying some nut shit like that and for even feeling like that! Examine the words a little. It's clear that he's hurt or was affected in some way or another, since he just referred to his child as "that" child. I get it, hurt people hurt people. But the one who gets hurt the most in this situation is the child having to grow up without everything he or she needs and deserves.

If you ever hear someone say something like that you most definitely need to look at him like he crazy, correct him, and tell him how wrong he is. Too many times we've heard something like this and said nothing at all. How will we correct this misconception if we sit around and say nothing and do nothing? If you're the one that thinks like that or says that I want you to think about your daughter being mistreated, hurt, raped, or killed because you made the decision to not be there to protect her because you didn't like how her mother handled situations or treated you! That's just it, once you father a child, it's no longer just about *you*. It's more about the child.

Now, I cannot let the mothers completely off scot free. Mothers play a big part in fatherhood or the lack of it. There's a misconception about the woman believing it's okay to knock, put down, or degrade the father to the child, in front of their child, or even loud enough for the child to hear. When you put the father down because of his shortcomings or because of your personal feelings toward him, you damage the child more than the father. Comments such as "Your dad isn't shit," or " Your father does this and that for his other children but not you," or "Your father is so sorry," all hurt the child's self-esteem.

What this does to our fatherhood? It does more harm than you can see, and just because you're mad. It's so wrong and hard for a man to come back from sometime. The effect that has on a child's mind are immense. Dads are supposed to be their children's heroes, so to hear Mom belittle Dad diminishes how the child sees his father. Mom says dad isn't shit, so she must be right because mom is always right, right? Who is the child supposed to side with? How is the child supposed to honor and respect their father and what he says after Mom beat him down so much? It changes the perception of what the child sees in her father! If Dad hurt Mom in any way, this is more reason for a child to rebel and not listen to the father because of the damage caused by the mother's words. It's easy for this to happen too. A lot of times a child is going to love mom the most and rightfully so, but you can't make fatherhood harder for the fathers, after knowing the history of our men and their pursuit of trying to understand and become a true father.

A lot of times than none the child will develop the same feelings toward dad as the mother has. Feelings are not necessarily reality, so this is not true in some cases. Sometimes I get it, us men as fathers fall way short of what we're supposed to be. Yet just because a relationship doesn't work out does not mean women have the right to use their bitterness to spoil any chance of a relationship with the father. That's just wrong and it affects us more then you know! The misconception of thinking that you The Mother can speak negative so freely about Dad and think it doesn't affect a man's fathering ability is also wrong!

If not corrected now, this practice will only add to our dysfunctional ways. It will continue to repeat the cycle of our unhealthy relationships, not just between parent and child, but between parents as well. Men are most certainly absent from their children's lives, at alarming rates, I might add. Mother and father are absent from each other's life as well. If we can change that situation, then we can begin to improve the fatherhood presence. Regardless of personal feelings or let downs, you sacrifice ya feelings for ya child. That's what love is: sacrifice. You two still have some things in common; if nothing else, you have the child or children! Why not sacrifice and be good friends between mother and father for your child? Fatherhood is one of the greatest things to happen to a man in this life. It's one of the greatest privileges and an honor as well.

As fathers, we must know and understand that if our children see us dishonor their mothers, they too will eventually do the same thing. Children do what they see. They will inherit the same trauma and behavior they see, and use it, if not toward their mothers then toward their girlfriends one day. When a boy sees abuse, he thinks, *this is what I'm supposed to do*. For the lil' girl that sees her mother being abused, she thinks she is supposed to take abuse. When these damaging conditions are inflicted upon us, history continues to repeat itself and fatherhood isn't looked at as a privilege and honor. Sometimes it's looked at as a burden. This is the perception that we must change. We must identify where this lack of excitement we sometimes see in our fathers arose. Life's beat downs sometimes stole our joy of being fathers.

One of the biggest misconceptions of fatherhood is this: Why is "mediocrity" okay with us fathers today? Is it because a lot of us grew up without fathers or proper fatherhood being displayed to us? Shouldn't not having dads have made us better dads? Seems like we should have been better dads because we knew what it felt like to miss certain things. We knew what it felt like to not have Dad to lean on or to show you how to do certain things. We knew what it felt like to not have your father be there for your basketball games, special days, or events. We never had a dad teach you or tell you the proper way to treat and talk to a young lady. For those reasons we always told ourselves we were going to be so much better than our dads! But this is where you must realize how low the bar has been set for us.

Listen to one of the examples of how we become so stagnant in our fatherhood. My father used to always say, "My father never did nothing for me but give me $30 and a sweatshirt for my 30th birthday." You gotta see how low that set the bar for me.

Him being deprived of so much from his father didn't set me up to do better. I'm sure my father said to himself, "I'm a be a much better dad then my dad was to me." But remember the bar was very low already. He didn't have a blueprint or road map on how to be a great dad or the direction to get there. When he became a father, his aim was to be better than his dad. That's what all fathers want: their sons to be better than them but, with the bar so low, it doesn't take much to be better than the guy who only ever gave you $30 and a sweatshirt.

My father definitely succeeded by being better than his dad. But did he get to a point of being better and just became content with the fact that he was better than his dad? The misconception in that is thinking was that a little bit better was enough.

Once I became a father, I definitely took notes on all the things my father did wrong. With that I figured I had all the information, know how, and experience to be a good father. My father did good at showing and displaying his love for his children, so I definitely made that a key element to my blueprint.

Remember that the bar I spoke about? Well, it wasn't as low as with my father's father, but it wasn't high either.

As I went through my progression as a father, I learned more and more things along the way. I displayed certain actions and characteristics that really led me to believe I was really a good dad!

I think of the moment I was finally able to be honest with myself and realize I wasn't a good dad or good enough! I was a selfish father, an ignorant father and, like my high school sweetheart and children's mother said a long time ago. I was "a good part-time dad" It took me a long minute to truly understand what she said and what she meant because of my bar being so low for fatherhood. Once I got a little past the bar that was set by my father, I thought it made me a good father.

I was a drug dealer that landed himself in jail with a 21-year sentence. I remember my mother telling me. "Them children don't need your money, they need you." I remember thinking, *yeah, right mom.* She just didn't understand the feeling I get leaving the mall with my son carrying four pairs of brand-new sneakers with the look on his face sayin', "I got the best father in the world!" Besides, I was lucky to get one pair of sneakers on a trip to the mall with my father, because my mom handled all that.

So that feeling I got added with the fact that I'm past the bar of fatherhood expectations and being better than my father has got to make me a good father, right? Wrong again! All I did accomplish was mediocrity. Why is mediocrity so okay with us today? It has a lot to do with the history of how we experience fatherhood and seeing it repeated over and over again. When I speak about our history I mean as far back as slavery. We've never really fully recovered from slavery. We've come pretty far but we didn't fully recover yet. We have to study our history in order to understand where we come from. That's the only way we know why things are this way and decide where we are going or should be going.

In short, as I said, dysfunctional fatherhood is linked back to our days as slaves. The damage still seeps out. We were set out on a course that we continue to follow and fall into to the present day. Black men were stripped of their manhood and fatherhood by stripping us of our natural roles as parents and protectors. What this did to black men was set things up, so they had to watch their women carry out the man's duties of providing for and protecting the children. It started way back then and it still goes on today. The misconception is that we think this is normal. We believe and think this is okay. That's why I said in the beginning of this book "...hear my experience and the experience of others that may challenge or change how you see things and how you approach things." You know I said it to recondition your mind some.

The aftermath of slavery was a serious blow to our concept of fatherhood. Black men were trying to find their way in a country that tried to make it hard on us at every turn. It even still goes on till this day. Just look at the laws and how they target us. They crush us within this system. Like I said before, "You got to know where you been in order to know where you're going or should be going." This is still their system that we have to work extra hard in to avoid inevitable failure since it was designed for our inevitable failure!

One in every ten black people are in prison on any given day. There are more black men in prison today than there were enslaved in 1850. Federal courts-imposed prison sentences on blacks that were 19% longer than those imposed on similarly situated white men.

What all this means is the attack on our fatherhood is REAL. From back then not allowing us to be the fathers, to the present day locking us up until after our children are grown, still not allowing us to be fathers. All the blame is not just on them, the system, or slavery. We have to take some responsibility. Now that we understand what we were and are up against, we cannot add to the destruction and dysfunction of us as fathers.

I'm not just talking to young fathers. I'm talking to all fathers. It doesn't matter if your children are young or already grown. We continually need to instill in them the true meaning of fatherhood and not be caught up in the misconceptions of what they "think" fatherhood is. So, if your son is grown, maybe it's not too late to get through to his children, and that way, to their children. If we do that, they won't have to suffer the same difficulties we did. No more half-dads or "part-time dads", we will produce whole, full on fathers.

Knowing our history should have us saying the hell with mediocrity because good is not always good enough. We should aim to be great and not just good because we know we have the ability and gifts to be great! Our history as fathers is just one more reason for us to push our children to be great, rather than just good. We can push them not to be content with a B when they can get an A. Been too many times that I heard fathers (and mothers) say to their child "...as long as you're passing." What the hell is that? It's us being okay with being average! This is just another example of how that bar of fatherhood has been so low for us. Our main concern is just if they are passing? If they are just getting by? That's not great, nor is that good fatherhood. We not gonna push our children to be the best or have the best? As parents, we be thinking we are doing a good job too. Even so, why settle for good when great is available?

Photo Gallery

An-Nisa   Quadir

Auanise, Journee, Laicie, Tyear. Me & Fareed Jr. – "2009"

Auanise, Journee, Tyear

Justice & Fareed Sr.

An-Nisa, Journee, Justice

Auanise, Laicie – "2004"

Journee, Me, Justice

Me, An-Nisa

Journee

Me & Justice

Fareed Sr. & Fareed Jr.

Karrie & Me   Laicie, Me, Tyson, Fareed Jr.

Lil Tariq & Big Tariq 2010

Quadir & Fareed

Laicie, Fareer, Tyear

Fareed

Tariq & Dad   Tariq age 12

Tariq age 12 & Fareed

Awards this Certificate in

Legal Assistant/Paralegal

with Distinction upon

Fareed T. Ray

who has fulfilled all the requirements prescribed by the School and is entitled
to all of the honors, rights and privileges thereunto appertaining.
In Testimony Whereof this recognition of achievement is

Given this 17th day of March 2020

President

Valerie L. Schule B.S., M. Ed.
Director of Education

The road to redemption …

Tyisha $ Fareed at Prom - "2001"

Laicie Ray's Graduation

CHAPTER 3

Being Da Man as Opposed to Being a Man

As far back as I can remember, I didn't aspire to be a real man. I wanted to be a real nigga. I wanted to be "Da Man". Where we come from, this is what we see as the goal by those in positions of power and influence. Being a man, you gotta know that you got a responsibility! If you're a natural born leader, you have a responsibility to lead! If you are very intelligent, you have a responsibility to help educate others. If you're strong and you are a good protector, then it's your job to step up and protect,

You can't be a leader by letting someone who's not a leader lead you! More times than none, they will lead you into a situation you cannot get out of or a situation you shouldn't have even been in! You're real sharp and intelligent, so you pick up on things easy. You have the ability to create and make something out of nothing. Instead, you just sit on all your good ideas, you don't share the knowledge, you don't even know that sharing knowledge is also your responsibility. You're not realizing that your knowledge and go-getter mentality and spirit will enable you and your family to get ahead in life. When it's in you, it's just in you. Let it out. You're not supposed to just sit idle and don't do nothing with it.

Of course, if you are a strong man or young man, you better never imitate a coward. As a man, it is your duty to protect your home and your family, as well as yourself. Martin Luther King, Jr. said, "If you haven't found something you'd die for, then you're not fit to live." Now, by no means am I saying start problems and get yourself killed. But as a man, you better be willing to stand up and protect you and yours!

So, let's break down and decipher being "Da Man" as opposed to being a man. For starters, you don't want to wake up in jail sentenced to life (or the reality that you're never getting out because you wanted to be "Da Man"). You don't want to wake up with HIV/AIDS. because you wanted to be "Da Man". You don't want your children to need you one day but you can't be there because being "Da Man" took you out of their lives permanently! You're not a man because a lot of girls like you. You're not a man because you hustle and can buy yourself some nice clothes or a car or even a house. You're not a man because you take care of others or pay their bills. You're most definitely not a man because you carry a gun and may even use it. It's not what you have or what you can give that makes you a man! It's who you *are*!

Growing up in the inner city, the 'hood, urban communities, if you possess some of these qualities and characteristics or all of them, you're definitely considered "Da Man". This is a heavy misconception where I come from. This misconception hinders a lot of us from being a real man rather than trying to imitate the one who thinks he's "Da Man". A lot of us swear we are leaders but, in reality, we are just followers. In part, it's because we do what we see, we follow what we see. Dare to be different sometime. You say you're a leader, right? You hate for someone to call you a follower even if you are in fact one! The truth hurts though. *Don't call me no follower because even if I am following, I still got potential to be a leader.* Then what are you waiting for? The time is now for you to change the story. You will make the story better because it is your story.

Once, me and my homie were having a conversation and we got

on the subject of my brother Tariq, may he rest in peace. Tariq lost his life to street violence on the fourth of July 2010. I told Homie how I used to always hear a voice in my head saying, "You're gonna save someone's life one day," but I couldn't save Tariq's. This is when my homie would say, "Man, that wasn't your fault." Yet, I saw things a little deeper than he did. I'm a leader. I'm a big brother. I have influence. I also have a responsibility to lead the Right Way if I truly am a leader! You see, you, me, and millions of other people are being misled. We miss vital points such as, if you become a lawyer, your little brother will want to become a lawyer. If you become a doctor that makes a lot of money and saves lives, there's a strong possibility that he'll want to be like his big brother and become a doctor, too. The first and strongest impressions come from what we see. That's how I know I could have made doing the right thing look just as cool as I made the wrong thing look cool, or so I thought. I was making the wrong thing look cool. This is why I always carried the guilt around with me, knowing I share the blame for losing my little brother, my heart. I know because I had that much power and influence.

Let me tell you how misled and deceived I was to EVERYTHING. Here's another quick story with a heavy message. I come home October 1, 2006, and my little brother Tariq couldn't wait to show me how he was a man, "Da Man". He gave me a couple hundred dollars and some drugs. He's just as tall as me, even built like me without jail weights. You know I asked him, "What you doing, Man?" His reply was "I'm out here, Bro'. When I came up here from Atlanta, I ain't really have nobody to look out for me. So, I had to do what 1 had to do." This story was so familiar. It sounded like my story, like so many other young men's stories at that age and their reasoning for doing what we be doing. Hustling, stealing, or robbing to make ends meet. Lack of guidance allows us to think and move like this. At that moment, I felt like: *who am I to tell him not to, knowing I'd do the same thing and did the same thing?* I should have been thinking about saving his life. But who would have known? I should have known! When we have little brothers and sisters, we must know we have a responsibility to lead and teach them the correct way. Instead, I showed him every wrong way you could go from way back when he was younger coming to visit. Even though I never showed him drugs or a gun, Ray Charles could see I was in the streets.

Back to the present, I'm looking at him like: *Fuck it, if he gonna be out here he might as well be where I could keep my eye on him and make sure he is alright. Besides, we were just trying to make some money, find our way and eventually step away from the game and do something else once we accumulated some real money.*

As I write this, a conversation my lady and I had prior to my October 1, 2006 release came to mind. I flat out told her that I'm coming home to get some money, but I only need around $200,000 and then, I'm out. Her reply was, "What if, right before you reach your goal, you end up going back to jail or worse, get killed out here?" I tried my best to convince her that nothing would happen. However, truth be told, in life — especially street life — you don't know what each day will bring your way. Yet, her words were supposed to make me think. A sign or messages always come to us, but a lot of times we refuse to listen or hear them.

Nobody could control me, so why would I think that I could control the narrative of how my little brother's life would go? As time went on, we had a little run, nothing major, but then he gets locked up, or should I say he gets set up? The setup was meant for me, actually. It was done by a dude that my father turned me on to, not on purpose but very carelessly. Result: Tariq goes to placement in juvie. During this time while Tariq's doing his bid, I turned it up a little bit. I bought myself a 2000 Range Rover. In 2007 I wasn't no bricklayer, but we came up from nothing. Therefore, it was progress like a motherfucker in his eyes. He is away doing good and I'm still being a bad leader. All he is thinking about is that he can't wait to come home and be back in the mix with his brother because his brother was "Da Man".

During this time, he sent me a letter one day. I'll never forget what he said in the letter, which looking back made me feel even worse after I lost him. He said, "You know how kids have idols when they growing up, like Emmitt Smith or Michael Jordan? Well, I ain't have no idols. You were my idol. You were like God to me." Even as I write this, ten years after his death, it still sucks a little life out of me because I feel as if I failed him! I didn't help educate him. I didn't guide him. I didn't show him nothing! I had so much influence and power and all I ever did was make being "Da Man" look so attractive, instead of being an actual man.

But you're strong, right? You're a leader, right? Where are we leading those that come after us? Are we leading them to death and destruction? Are we not even giving them a chance at success? But we love them? *You are strong. You are a leader. You love them, or do you?* This is what you gotta ask yourself and be real with yourself about. Do I really love my little brothers and sisters, or do I love my desires more? *Do I even know what love is? Do I even know what being a man means?*

I'm so driven to get this book and my stories out there, so that I can maybe right some of my wrongs. When I do, maybe some people like me can sit down, think, and listen to the signs. Am I going down the right road? What will this cost me? What will this cost those around me, those who love me, those who need me? Something I may say might make someone think, may curb someone's actions, and could create a better outcome for him or her. Someone wouldn't have to think," What if I would have done this or said that."

I replay July 4th, 2010 in my mind so many times, thinking how I could have changed things that night. That night we were supposed to go down to a strip club in Baltimore. As we sat at his baby mother's family's cookout, it was getting late, so I asked him, "We going or what?" His reply was, "We can go tomorrow. Tomorrow's another day," Tomorrow never came for him. You know, I beat myself up saying I could have changed things if I would have just said, "No, let's go tonight." I think back to what I could have done that night. Did I miss something I could have said or did that night? In fact, it was long before that night that I could have tried to change the narrative. On many occasions, I had seen how much influence and power I had, I could have sacrificed my desires and began to let something else look attractive to him other than what I was doing.

Remember, I was his idol. So, whatever I did, he would have loved and wanted to do too. To be an effective and good leader, you must be aware of who you're leading, who's watching and looking up to you. You must also know where you're leading them. If you don't you could be leading them and yourself to y'all's demise!

"The man who plays it safe by not seeming to care too much so he can avoid the painful risk of losing, is only half a man."

Hardest loss, R.I.P. Bro…

Tariq and his mother   Tariq Sr. and Tariq Jr.

Tariq At The Airport 2010

Tariq and friends

CHAPTER 4

Females and Our Relationships with Them

A boy or man's status sometimes is measured by how many girlfriends he has. This is a misconception that found us long before we found the female or had any relationship at all.

As one of the most important misconceptions, we must look at and try to re-evaluate it. This misconception changes how we see things, changes how we act, and completely depreciates the over-all value we have for females.

Take a look at the value the average boy or man places on his mother and daughters. It would be World War III if someone disrespected a boy's or man's mother or daughter. For example, take how many school fights occurred because someone said something about another's mother. Punches were thrown, even though the mother wasn't even known to the one who made the comment. Yet, it's a well-known fact, the "value" we place on our moms. It's so much a fact that if you called someone ugly and they said "Ya mother," it was enough to provoke a fist fight because of the value and love we have for our mothers. They are our everything, and in most cases, our only thing. Then when you mention our daughters. Over our moms we will get into a fight in a heartbeat, but for our baby girls, our princesses, we will kill and die for! You better not upset, make mad, or put a finger on our girls. This highest level of love and value we have reserved for our little girls and women-to-be. Still, when it comes to women in general, we don't care nearly as much. Ask yourself why that is. I mean, we want a certain level of love, respect, and honor for our moms and daughters but for the rest of the females we fall short.

Before I go on, let me give you a few examples of how we interpret these values of womanhood incorrectly and also our relationships with them. Look at where it first started or where we first saw this misconception to understand why so many relationships fail before they start. To know why so many relationships are so toxic going in we must first understand the origin of these issues or misconceptions. We need to know what causes relationships to fail, what seeds were planted, and then hopefully, we can change this misconception. If we continue believing it's the correct way of thinking and seeing things, we'll never do it right. It starts so early in our youth.

As kids, how many times did we witness a friend, peer, or even ourselves being considered cool because three different girls liked this particular boy? Yes, we may look at this as being innocent and harmless, but this is where some of the misconception begins. One may take this misconception along with them throughout life. So, it may have started out innocent and harmless but as you get older, and you say, "I got three girlfriends and they know about each other and they aren't letting me go despite the fact." That's when harmless begins to affect other young ladies now. It's about high school time when others see this, and it begins to be a competition thing amongst young boys. It's a young boy's nature to want to compete and be better than the next guy. Now we have numerous boys with numerous girlfriends. The young females are the ones that get the short end of the stick. They resort to bending and having to compete with these other "girlfriends" because they desire the attention and love of this boy that they like. In fact, these young boys aren't even able to cherish, respect, or love these females yet because, in most cases, they have yet to learn how. Let's ask ourselves, why is that? Why does a young man enter into his adulthood not know about the basic essentials of liking or loving a female, i.e., his girlfriend?

One reason is that single-parent households are at an all-time high. In the majority of these single-parent instances, it's the woman, the female that's raising the kids by herself. Often, she's raising boys to be men. No disrespect to the moms, but are they able to teach us the proper way to treat a female that we like or love? Moms can tell us this is how you are supposed to do and be. But it's the example of the men in our lives that influence us the most. It's the fathers, grandfathers, uncles, brothers, and older cousins, and the men who stand in for them that we can relate to. It's these men that should take on the responsibility of teaching our young boys the correct way.

Moms can tell us, but men must *show* us. By seeing Dad cherish Mom, adore her, make her smile and be happy; a boy will want to do as he sees being done. If a boy doesn't have a dad around, then maybe Pop-Pop or their uncle can show him. But if a boy has no one teach him the right way, then he's subjected to learning the wrong way.

Too many kids and young boys are growing up fast with too much access to things they shouldn't be able to see or know about. Take movies for example. A young boy sees a movie about pimps and players and the images he gets from these types of movies will most likely have an enormous impact and influence — greater than we actually realize. These characters are seen with the best cars, jewelry, and clothes. In some of these movies the characters are shown hitting and smacking their females. A young boy should never be able to see or witness this type of behavior until he has a healthy respect for women. Not only do they see this in movies, but they might sometimes capture and experience these realities in their own households. Instead of seeing Dad love, cherish and adore his mother a boy sees him making her cry from physical or emotional abuse, or both. When this type of behavior becomes common, the chances are this little boy will grow up someday to do some of the things he has seen while growing up.

These misconceptions are real. A young boy thinks it's okay to put his hands on his girlfriend just to let her know who's the boss or because maybe she did something disrespectful and he's seen Dad do it." Or even in some instances, he's seen characters in movies do it. I'm speaking from personal experience. I saw it in my household, in the movies, and even witnessed it looking out my front door. I've seen not just the physical abuse, but the mental abuse, as well as the overall lack of respect for females. I'm pretty sure that I'm not the only one that grew up seeing and learning these types of things as an adolescent. The things that transcended into our minds gave us the idea that these wrong behavior patterns were really okay for us to do.

In 1991 the movie New Jack City came out and there was a scene that stayed with me when the character Nino Brown hit his girlfriend and dumped champagne on her head. He said, "Cancel this bitch, I'll get another one." Imagine a young boy seeing this and what it does to his mind and how it can affect how he treats women. Twenty something years later, Lil Wayne rapped the lyrics, "Had to cancel that bitch like Nino," Still negatively depicting our females all these years later, he glamorized this scene in the movie. The same scene that left a lasting impression in my mind as a kid back then. Could this have added to my lack of respect for our women? Most certainly it did, and it does to so many others.

That kind of stuff teaches us that we don't have to respect or value women. The only exceptions to the rule are when it comes to your mother. sister, or daughters. Those situations are different because we don't want anybody else disrespecting them. Yet, if one is not careful and does not learn to change his ways, "Karma"(What goes around, comes around) may reverse the role being played to become that your mother, sister, or daughter is being treated how you treated others!

The majority of everything that we see shows man not giving the female her due. This is a big problem because we are conditioned to think that there is nothing wrong with that behavior. Unless we learn to get a new outlook on this matter, that attitude just becomes second nature for us young men like it was for the many generations before us and will be for those that come after us.

Not to make this a religious conversation but the majority do believe in God, whether you be Muslim, Christian, Jewish, or another belief system. Let us understand our Creator's reason for creating man and woman. The purpose was to worship and give thanks to God, of course. Man was created first and woman was created from man's rib. I believe that's how the story goes in most of the religious teachings. Women were a gift for man, in a sense, created so we would have company and create more little boys and girls. Yet women are not always treated like the gifts they are.

My lady and I always have deep conversations, real conversations. My past behavior and actions tend to come up. She may say, "If you love me so much, why did you do this or that?" or "Why weren't you romantic?" She said it so many times, questioning my behavior, that I began to ask myself why I did certain things. I first made light of the situation and told her the snake and the hiker story. The hiker took the hurt snake down the mountain. The hiker told the snake, "I know that you'll bite me if I do, and the snake replied, "I promise I won't." So, upon arriving down the mountain, sure enough the snake bit him. The hiker jumped back and said, "I thought you said that you would not bite me!" The snake replied, "You knew what I was before you picked me up." I'm thinking she got it. I was saying, "This is who I was when you met me." Instead, she said, "You are going to compare yourself to a snake?" Once that scenario was not going to fly, I really had to think about all the events that led us to this point. All the things I've seen and done. That's when the answers came to me.

Her asking me, "Would you want someone to treat your daughter the way you treat me?" She made me think and with that, this chapter was born. For me to answer her would help her understand that is what made me.

Answering these questions may also help others change some of their ways, as well as how they see the incorrect way of thinking. This got me on the whole misconception thing because of the things we were exposed to — thing that a lot of times made us think it was okay to put your hands on a woman, or that it is ok to use women, or that it's ok to lie, cheat, and deceive a woman. Sometimes you were even considered cool if you did these things.

Think of the guy you heard say, "Oh, I just be using her for her crib," or "…to do this or that," or "I got a wife, a chick, and a rida," It's sad but true that this is how many boys and men think about women. They think this is acceptable. All these things are learned behaviors because life is what you're exposed to. Now take this into consideration: if this was happening to your mother would it still be considered cool?

Over the early years of my life, this is some of what I saw. This is some of what I was exposed to. In return, this too is some of what I became. It wasn't just me. It's millions of young boys being exposed to it and then so many also become "me". Whether you display one of these misconceptions or all of them, you too have added to the problems.

Someone asked me before, "Would you want your daughter to be with a guy like you?" My reply was, "With a heart like mine, I wouldn't mind because eventually he is going to get it right." They looked at me like I was crazy and said, "Be real with yourself!" That's when it hit me, and I said, "Hell, NO! I don't want them to experience the type of hurt and pain I put my girls' mothers through.

These misconceptions have been going on so long that they begin to transfer over to women. They, i.e., women, begin to take on the role of a man. It doesn't just happen to women even though it's more common for the man to display these misconceptions on a daily basis. However, more and more women are trying to catch up to the men that share these views. A lot of women put the shoe on the other foot now. It's another example of a crazy misconception thinking, "He love me because he put his hands on me," or "He's just crazy in love with me." But that's just it! This is not love at all.

These misconceptions continue to be some of the main reasons our relationships fail before they even start, the reasons our relationships are so toxic. Look at the number of women who commit suicide or even that killed their spouse due to domestic violence.

Again, life comes from what you're exposed to. You see these things, the behaviors on television, in your community, or even in your household, to the point they seem to be normal. Then the likelihood is that you believe this is okay for you to do as well.

Growing up, who were our examples of a good man? If you had none, then this may add to the reasons your relationships seem to fail. It is so much easier to conform, when children see what it looks like to cherish and love a woman, especially their mothers, by the father or stepfather, etc. We've got to allow our children to see us better as a whole.

Now ask yourself *why* it is so important for us to try to change these misconceptions. Then ask yourself *how* do we change them?

Let me start by saying that there is no figure that has been oppressed and underappreciated as much as females have been, especially the black female. Yes, we've come a long way from a time when women didn't have as many rights as they always should have, such as being able to vote or not being able to wear pants to school. Regardless, we still have so far to go with how we see and treat females! If we don't this misconception will continue to be one of the reasons our relationships fail and will continue to hinder so many of our youth, especially in our urban communities where certain things are looked at as being cool or okay.

Things being "interpreted incorrectly is what misconception means. It starts with our own mother. You love, honor, and cherish your mother and you should try to apply that same respect, thoughtfulness, and honor with every female that enters your world, your life. This philosophy or way of interacting gives each encounter an opportunity to always be peaceful, nice, and meaningful, whether it's just an opportunity to be friends with a female or she's a potential girlfriend. This could one day become our universal way of treating and dealing with females. If this can happen, it ensures us that our daughters, sisters, granddaughters, their kids and even their kids' kids won't have to deal with the lack of respect being so common.

One day, I was on the phone arguing and after I hung up the phone, my then-girlfriend asked, "Who was that?" I said, "My mother." That's when she said, "If you don't have a good relationship with ya mother, chances are you won't have a good relationship with your girlfriend." In my situation, I found this to be true, because I didn't have a good relationship with my mom until recently. Until my mother and my relationship came full circle, I didn't truly begin to understand my mother's love. Then, I began to be able to honor, love, and respect everything she had to say. As a result, my relationship and bond with my lady began to get better as well.

Understanding this misconception can change the course of our relationships. This is why it's so important to change these misconceptions. One of our main objectives is to change the course of our relationships and see to it that they become successful. In order to do that, we must know the right way. They say, "Money makes the world go around." That may be true in a sense but know this: you and I wouldn't be in the world if it wasn't for a woman. There is only one way for a man to be born, and that's through a woman. If it wasn't for women then there wouldn't be birth, our gifts to mankind.

Falsehood and misconception have always destroyed empires, so it definitely can destroy individuals and families. We begin to change these misconceptions by uncovering the truth. Not allowing our youth to continue to do all kinds of blind following, not truly understanding why they're even following the behaviors they have seen. We must make them conscious of what really moves their emotions and compels them to behave in healthy, productive ways rather than not moving in a certain way just because they see it. As people, we oftentimes have been susceptible to the ways around us that compel all kinds of behavior on our part. We do it because we are consciously or unconsciously imitating others. So, the solution ultimately goes back to us being better examples from Day One. By the time a child is seven years old, over 80% of what he or she knows is from what they hear or see. Sometimes we are teaching without being aware that we are teaching. What a child sees and hears from us sometimes, we may not even notice the child is listening or seeing. This is when a child learns to think wrong is right because he or she saw adults do it. Their impressionable minds take in and record what they see and hear — TV, movies, and rap video, for example. We have seen kids imitate or want to be like what they see. That means we must give guidance to help them separate what's real from what's fake. Inside our family life, Dad must show love for Mom because what Dad shows is real, he's my hero. If we can't be examples or give better guidance with our actions and monitoring what they see and hear at young ages, chances are they will learn wrong attitudes! By showing how and monitoring them we give them a better chance not to fail, and we will never have to feel like we failed them!

Our children, our nephews, nieces, and grandkids will begin to get better when we show them how. The times of the past and now will begin to be frowned upon, because we instill in them how to value females and our relationships with them.

CHAPTER 5

Work Ethic or the Lack of It

Work Ethic: belief in work as a moral good! I got to start this chapter off with a quick question. Say you have two ways to get to the mall from your house. One road takes about 20 minutes. Another road only takes about 12 minutes; it's a shortcut. Taking the shortcut is a small risk because you have to ride through a bad neighborhood. Which road will you take? Mostly everyone in life is trying to save time and would take a shortcut. Everyone wants to take a shortcut at one time or another in their lifetime! Some of us ALWAYS want to take the shortcut!

A lot of us, and I don't say "us" lightly because we know who we are. A lot of us can't stand to even think of having to work hard or just work the factory or warehouse job. A lot of us growing up in the 'hood never aspired to work in the factory, we viewed that as one of the bottom-of-the-food-chain jobs, a last resort thing! Especially when we aspire to get rich fast, we think of being a rapper, athlete, or drug dealer. The factory job is the job for "I just got out of jail, I'm in the halfway house and I need something right away to be able to come out of the halfway house." There's very little commitment or love for doing that job.

Let me back up some. Why is a factory or warehouse job viewed in that way? Let's be honest, it's because it's not glamorous to us. At a day and age when everything has to be attractive, we want to be able to win today, look fly today. Why? That's because tomorrow isn't promised, anyway. So why do I have to wait, and then just wait to be able to live paycheck to paycheck? Besides, "the working man is a sucker," right? Wrong, and I plan on giving you the answer for why the working man is not a sucker.

Remember, all these misconceptions got us twisted and lost. The misconceptions are a part of the reason why we are coming in last place in the race. When I say "we" I mean black people! I'll touch on that a little later but let me stick to the subject at hand. Our work ethic or lack of it is at an all-time low, Why? That's because instead of working hard to achieve things, going through the process, moving up at our jobs, we feel as though if we can outthink others and take a shortcut, then we don't have to work hard or take the long way! It's so embedded in our brains that when we speak to each other and someone says, "What's up?" You say, "Taking it easy." Then the first one says, "That's the only way to take it, the easy way." Is this just a figure of speech? No, it is not! From early in our life this was conditioned in our minds and became a way of life for so many of us. Why work hard when I can get it easy or in other words "take it easy." Do you know what this leads to?

It leads to a lot of us cutting corners, cutting each other's throats in a race to take what the next man got. Whether that be his woman, his money, his power, or his attention, it's sad to say we are like crabs in a bucket. As soon as we see one getting to the top, we will pull his ass back down with us in the bucket. We rarely can be happy for each other when someone makes it. That is why I earlier said, "We are coming in last in the race." My homie told me one day, "Yo, long as you're not doing better than a person, it isn't a problem but the minute you start doing better than them, then it's a problem." He was kicking some knowledge. We were at the bar. I had just come home from prison and people was coming up to me left and right just saying" What's up?" I'm brand new to the streets again. Couple of ladies stopping by to say, "Hi. Welcome home!" After the last group walked away, Homie leans over and says, "I'm a be ya competition when I get off house arrest and can come out regularly." I said to myself: *Wow, first he told me and then he showed me. As long as you're not doing better than a person it isn't a problem, but the minute you start doing better than them, then it's a problem.* He couldn't take it that I was getting more attention than him. It's just one example of my point about what this mentality and misconception leads to! This thinking brings destruction among us, which holds us back, keeps us last in the race! When our work ethic or lack of it leads us to take the easy route, and we find the easy route isn't really easy at all. It leads us to want to take what's not ours, to robbery, stealing, and worse. Then that leads to jail and sometimes death if we try to jack the wrong person. How many times you heard about a guy getting killed trying to rob someone? All this comes from us NOT having a good work ethic. No one wants to work hard to achieve their goals and plans. We want it easy and fast — a short cut!

Early in life, it should be our primary focus to condition our children's minds to work hard and have a good work ethic. We should teach them to avoid the free lunch, because this can add to them being lazy and wanting something for nothing. Most things we think are free, aren't really free at all. Most times they come with a price! We should teach them that sometimes you get what you pay for, most of the time you get less, almost never do you get more then you paid for. This mind set helps them to avoid some of the pitfalls that come with taking the short cut, the easy route, or the freebie. Things aren't just given. Most times, they come with a price, you just have to ask yourself if you're willing to pay that price!

I remember seeing the classic movie *A Bronx* Tale (Savoy Pictures, 1993). The kid in the movie said something that would stick with me for a long time. The kid, "C", said to his father, "The working man is a sucker, Dad." His father was a bus driver, working hard to provide for his family. Little C liked to mimic the gangsters that hung down the street from his house, the way they walked, the way they talked, and even the way they did their hand gestures. So naturally, when Little C heard the gangster character, Sonny, who he admired the most, say, "The working man is a sucker," he took that to heart as if it was law. I mean, why wouldn't he? The perception, the visual, was that Sonny was winning, right? You be the judge of this once I dial it back some.

Other things that steal work ethic from us before we ever get a chance to inherit a good work ethic are the things we see on TV. When I saw that movie at like 10 years old and he said, "The working man is a sucker," that left a lasting impression in my mind. We see things like that in a movie. and we look out our front doors to see guys on the corner fresh as shit with new clothes, sneakers, hats, and jewelry on. Then, you look at the hardworking man living on ya street and he don't have much. He got a car that seems to always be breaking down, his clothes aren't the best. You think about that statement, "The working man is a sucker," and it appears that the statement definitely has some truth to it. You begin to buy into this statement, you really begin to believe it. Then, you, too, would rather take the easy route. Why work hard when it appears, we won't make it far? These thoughts kill our work ethic before we can even get it started.

Lack of work ethic leads us to think the world owes us something! This has to be one of the most detrimental misconceptions for us. The world doesn't owe you anything! The world is your playground, *you* owe it to yourself. You owe it to yourself to give yourself a chance. A good work ethic and hard work gives you the opportunity to achieve all your goals and dreams. Know that the easy route, the shortcut can be an illusion, so one shouldn't be so quick to take it and not want to work for whatever it is that you seek to have.

Me and my peers sat back having a conversation not too long ago. By my peers, I mean men in jail with me, men that used to think like me, men who were deceived by the same misconceptions that deceived me. Some are still deceived by the same misconceptions. Truth be told, everyone won't get it. Everyone won't share or obtain the same knowledge and wisdom. But a lot will. A lot will grow and mature with the right guidance.

As me and my peers sat and talked about how we used to think and see things, we realized the importance of work ethic and what ultimately led us all to jail, how all things intertwined with each other for this result. Whether you robbed to get here or stole to get here, they were all fueled by the same misconception with the goal to get ahead and get ahead quick with little to no work.

On any given day, the combined years total of those among us having these conversations, would exceed over 100 years, easy. Between us, 100 years had to be served before we could all be free. When they look back, most people with such harsh realities wish they could go back and do some things, if not all things, differently. But there's no going back. You're stuck with what you're stuck with. This is when the statement, the belief in the statement "The working man is a sucker," don't seem so true or cool after all. The working man done moved up in his job, made it a career with promotions, to get good money now. The working man built his home. The working man started a nice family, and in some cases, the working man made our girlfriends their wives and are raising our children. Plus, the working man is free! From where me and my comrades sit, it's clear to see the working man is winning, and our belief in that misconception made us lose and lose big! We would trade places with the working man in a heartbeat. After losing so much, we finally realize the working man isn't a sucker after all. The working man was smart, the working man was patient, the working man is a winner, big time! A few people still think contrary to this, but they are the fools! You don't have to be one any longer!

Diploma Picture here

The road to redemption for me had already started because it was mental. When I told myself that I was gonna make those who love me be able to be proud of me it started; that made it tangible. I could begin to see and feel my efforts and intentions.

Picture 19

Two and a half years later, after the first appeal was denied, my 2255 motion was granted. A 2255 is where they said you do have merits to your case and issues to be fixed. *You mean to tell me my prayers, hard work, and perseverance is about to pay off?*

CHAPTER 6
Commitment

Commitment! What is that? I asked my eleven-year-old daughter, "What is commitment or what does it mean to be committed?" Her reply was, "I know what it means but I can't describe it." I said to her, "You have to know the true meaning behind a word, in order to be able to fulfill it. How will you be able to be committed to school, work, and one day, your husband and children if you don't know the true meaning of the word commitment?"

Commitment is a pledge to do something. It's an obligation to a particular thing and/or person. it means you have a duty to do something. In other words, it is being "ALL in", focused on what you're committed to.

How many times have we called ourselves committed to something, just to later realize we weren't nearly as committed as we should have been? Commitment is a bigger deal than we realize. Commitment brings about excellence! So, the misconception that commitment is not that important is a big mistake. Early in a child's life, he or she should be taught to understand just how important commitment and being committed are to the success in each of our lives. Again, commitment brings about excellence. It brings excellence in your relationship, your career, raising your children, and just everyday life, period.

Look at NBA star Kobe Bryant (R.I.P to the Black Mamba). This man was so committed. He was dedicated to his commitment to be the best he could be at the sport he loved. His commitment brought forth so much success and happiness, not just for himself, but for his family, those around him, and so many to come after him. This one person's commitment opened so many doors for so many people. The effect he has had on little girls wanting to play basketball is profound. Because he had all girls and no boys, he was so committed to push his daughters, other little girls wanting to play basketball, and to keep pushing women's basketball forward. He pushed so that his middle school girls' basketball team beat a middle school boys' basketball team. This is what commitment brings. The ability to break barriers!

NFL quarterback Michael Vick showed two different types of commitment that we could learn from. Michael Vick was committed to being the best quarterback and breaking the barriers placed on black quarterbacks, and his commitment enabled him to do so. Michael Vick was from my era and was, in my opinion, the best college football player I've ever seen. But the second part of his commitment is what intrigued me the most. His commitment and dedication also sparked a fire within me, which made me committed to want to be like Mike.

See, Michael Vick made some bad decisions and it literally cost him everything. Can you imagine going from being one of the best in the game, doing things no other quarterback ever did, being the highest paid player in the game to being a federal inmate just like me? He was sitting where I sit right now for his role in the dog fighting and animal cruelty case that the federal government charged him with. Even though Michael and I both come from similar environments, due to bad decisions we both were subject to failure. However, I saw Michael Vick recommit to fixing things, righting his wrongs. He recommitted to not only being a great football player but also a great man showing others another commitment to educate people about animal rights. His commitment to being such a stand-up man was so strong that when he lost it all, his money and property along with gaining a ton of debt, he could have filed bankruptcy and been clear of the rest of the debt. Instead, he said he would repay EVERYTHING he owed. Due to his commitment to succeed and win, as well as be a better man that made better decisions, he did just that. He won big time! He paid back all the money he owed, made more money, and kept his word, going above and beyond to educate others and become an activist for animal rights. None of this happens without a certain level of commitment to staying true to who he was and what he said, his pledge, his obligation, his duty, and being "all in". Like I said, his commitment sparked something in me to want to be even more committed to my goals and purpose. Look what can happen when we display this type of commitment and dedication.

This is why I believe we should spend more time and energy teaching our young ones about commitment and what it truly means to be committed. At what age should we begin to instill in our kids, nieces, and nephews the true meaning of this word? In my opinion, five, six, or seven are the ages when we should begin to drive this home with them. These are the ages where a child will begin to want to get involved in dance, sports, music, instruments, and more. So, this is when we sit them down and explain to them how they need to be committed if they are going to get involved. If some children don't find interests in these other activities, they still need to learn the importance of school and understand their commitment to learning. They need to know and understand that they HAVE to be committed to school, and they have to see it through to the end. The best way to assure that is to make sure they understand commitment on every level. Not just school, sports, career, etc., but they must understand it all around the board. This will give them a better chance at success because they will always be committed to what they do.

My opinion on what age and how we instill this in our youth doesn't have to be absolute. However, know that at some point we do NEED them to understand commitment, as well as the lack of commitment. Where I went wrong, I believe, was thinking I could be committed to two different things at the same time. Yet, how could I be fully committed to both and get the best out of me in both? I'm not saying it cannot be done, I'm just saying I couldn't do it. In some of these instances, you will have divided loyalties that will most times conflict with one another. More times than none, my mistake was thinking that I could spread myself thin and do it all. The misconception of thinking we can be committed to too many things at the same time doesn't just revolve around relationships, it hits a wide range of things.

When I met my first love, it was "love at first sight". I mean it was "a match made in heaven". Some people question love at first sight. Don't, because I felt it, so I know it is possible. Then, I met my second love. That wasn't love at first sight, but my second love was a bad mother lover too. I mean, my second love touched me in ways I never knew before. My second love gave me power.

My father introduced me to my first love in 1986. I had to be around five years old, and he gave me my first football. Football was my very first love. I took that ball everywhere with me. I couldn't get enough of it. When it was hot outside, and even when it was freezing out, you would catch me playing with my football. Then, my father signed me up to play for the Harrisburg Packers and I did my thing. I did it so well that my dad used to sit with folks and brag about how well I played. If I loved football before, seeing the effect on my father (my hero) made me really in love with football then. I saw that my success could make not only me happy but my family happy too. Through football, I could also get a scholarship to go to college and maybe make a lot of money playing the sport I loved. This had to be the easiest decision I'd ever have to make. It was nothing for me to commit and stay committed to my first love, my dream! No one had to set this dream up for me or put it in my head. It was my dream from Day One. It would be nothing for me to be committed, or so I thought.

As the years went on, I maintained my love for football, but I kind of just went with the flow. I think I relied too much just on God-given talent, so I lacked commitment to get better, stronger, and faster. Still, I was able to turn heads. On the other hand, when I look back twenty-four years ago, I realize my commitment wasn't where it needed to be if this was truly going to be my dream.

This is where I had to really examine my commitment. Did I even understand what it truly meant to be committed? Was I just like my daughter, when she said to me, "I know what it means but I can't describe it"? Is this what they mean when they say history repeats itself? It most certainly will if we don't stop the cycle with proper parenting and teaching of essential things, such as commitment. Your commitment can be the determining factor in your failure or success!

In 1994, I was formally introduced to my second love, the streets! Even though my first love had my heart, my second love dazzled the shit out of me. I remember walking home from practice seeing all the hustlers in the hood, nice chains on, nice clothes, fresh to death. They had the girls hanging on the corners with them and all. As we'd walk by, they might stop us and be like, "What's up, little man? When's y'all next game? We gonna come to the game, if you score two touchdowns, I'm gonna give you some money. Stick with that shit, go to college and make it to the pros." They gave us young dudes hope in their words, but they also gave us hope in their actions. What I was chasing — college, being a star, attention, respect, money, girls, and overall notoriety — obtaining them was close to ten years away. I could get most of these things from the streets, now. With that, the seed was planted!

During football season, everything was beautiful, going to school maintaining good grades to be able to stay on the team and be eligible, and hanging out at the coach's house. But once the season was over, here came the distractions. Now, with no real guidance, how will a child survive the temptations and allure of the streets? Me, I figured I could have it all, enjoy my commitment to football *and* begin my commitment to the streets. My stubbornness to remain in both led to eventual lack of commitment overall. What I'm saying is that when we don't offer guidance, we don't even give our youth a chance. See, this commitment thing goes further than being committed to a sport. That's just one of the easiest examples I use for a young person to be able to identify with.

Lack of commitment is also when a father walks out on his family. A mother is left, not knowing how to raise a thirteen-year-old boy who suddenly begins to act more and more rebellious due to the disappointment and betrayal he feels towards his father and his father's departure. Mom can't really handle her son, nor does she understand what her son is going through or feeling. Mom is dealing with her own pain of losing her husband, the only man she loved and thought she knew. Her son reminds her of the pain that her husband inflicted. It's easier for her to let go, kick him out, and just focus on her other children. *Besides,* she thinks, *her son will get out there, see how hard it is, then come back and appreciate his mother and all she gives.* But will he? When there comes a "fork in the road", he thinks he is going right (to the streets) because he's strong enough to survive the streets. He does not know he just went left and will continue this path for years to come. It started in the household, with the lack of commitment. A man is supposed to be the leader. Dad is strong! He's the one that's supposed to protect and hold everything together. Now, it seems like more and more the role is being reversed. The women lead! The women are the strong ones. We witness them doing everything a man is supposed to be doing. They stick and stay because of their men's lack of commitment to stick and stay. Instead, we men leave and flee! What guidance does such a man give this thirteen-year-old boy as he moves closer to manhood? What commitment does he show? None at all! This is what we gotta see and change. It's not just about the man or woman. It's about the child's best interest and being committed to his future success.

The lack of commitment is widespread and shown to our youth all too often. When do we see Dad, Uncle, or older brothers stay committed (no matter what) for the greater good of the family? We see it less and less. How will you know something about commitment when no one ever showed you what it means to be committed in a relationship? Growing up, what if you had seen your father have other girlfriends on the side when he was married to your mother? More times than none, we will do as we've seen done because we think it's okay. However, one must be careful, for there's a word, reciprocity and it means "what goes around comes around", just like karma means. If you can't be committed, then don't expect someone else to be committed to you when you want or need it most. You may get it, but you might not. Just know commitment is not owed to you. Karma, remember? Karma may be owed to you! These examples are just two ways commitment can help you and others — or hurt you and others!

You get out what you put in. In order to be great, you have to be committed to greatness, no matter what you think greatness is: Sports, relationships, career, or school. God-given talent sometimes just is not enough! God-given talent, wisdom, knowledge is given to millions. What will set you apart from others? Hopefully, your commitment will, because it's those who stay fully devoted to hard work, drive, and sacrifice that will be the ones who achieve their dreams and goals. I learned the hard way about distractions and not having the ability to be fully committed to my craft. It only led me to jail, getting flag football championships and telling the younger guys about what I used to be.

See, this is not just my story, but the story of many of our black people's story as well. The stories affect us in more ways than we care to realize because, if we cared to truly realize it, we would begin to change the narrative. We see the issues; we have identified some of the problems. What will we do to change it? This is not just a question for the adults, this is a question for the teenager who's starting to go through some of these problems or issues. Knowing the answer will better you for your son, daughter, little brother, or little sister.

This commitment thing stretches far and wide. One of the first things you want to teach your children, siblings, nieces, or nephews is how to be committed and why it's so important.

"If you're committed to someone, you don't allow yourself to find perfection in someone else." – many authors take credit for this, but it is best known from the 2014 Chris Evans movie, *Before We Go.*

CHAPTER 7
Asking for Help

The misconception that asking for help means you are weak is definitely one we black men should pay more and closer attention to. This misconception is one that's been holding us back for a long time without us being fully able to understand how much it affects us. Do we understand all the issues that are linked to this one misconception? Do we understand when the misconception usually starts? Do we understand why it starts? Not asking for help when you really need it can lead to mental health issues, suicide, "wild child syndrome" or just not knowing how to fulfill your obligations as you come of age. When does this misconception usually start?

In today's world, some children can be very cruel to other children. I mean, they can be downright vicious. As parents or older siblings, it is our job to be sensitive to our children's feelings and views. I say that because, as a man and father, one of the first things I was to my son was tough. This is a very common trait for some of us fathers. We instill in our sons' things like: "Man, stop crying!" "Don't be no cry baby." "You're tough," and more. I get it, we definitely want our boys to grow up big and strong. We want that especially in the world today when they *shall* meet many challenges growing up black. Plus, we want them to be able to look out for their siblings. We also want them to look out for their mothers one day if needed in our absence (because our absence has become so normal — but that's a story for another page). Those over-tough traits happen when we over-instill not being weak in our sons. We've made it so that a little boy believes he has to be strong on all cylinders all the time. It's to the point he believes if he asks for help, it indicates that he's weak! Therefore, he will never ask for help, even when he really needs it, even when his life or death depends on it. This most certainly can lead to a child having mental health issues or possibly becoming suicidal one day for the child that really needs help and never gets it. They carry certain things around with them to the point they can't take it no more and it, literally, destroys them. This doesn't just take place from the fathers to the sons. That was just an example of how it can happen from my own misconceptions. It's many different variables that all lead to the same destructive outcomes and behaviors. It's the daily pain that one may carry with him if he doesn't understand that it's not only okay, but also, it's necessary to ask for help when you need it. In fact, psychiatrists, psychologists, pastors, rabbis, imams, and smart leaders recommend asking for help. As fathers or father figures it's our job to be in tune with our children. It's our job to make them comfortable enough to want to ask us for help when it comes to anything.

Sometimes a child also gets caught up in the misconception that, even if he asks for help, nobody will run to him or save him. Think about the children being mistreated, molested, or raped. They're misled by the misconceptions related to asking for help; they keep bad treatment to themselves and never ask for help. It weighs them down so much that some will turn into a "wild child", partying all the time, doing drugs, sex, anything to escape the pain without having to ask for or get the right help. If they'd done it a long time ago it may have helped them cope better. Then of course, you also have some that carry it inside, trying to forget, but they can't. These often end up committing suicide. These situations are the reality of too many of our people, and it's all because we haven't done enough to change the misconception that asking for help equals weakness.

Asking for help doesn't mean you are or make you weak. Asking for help doesn't mean you're dumb. I spoke about kids being cruel because they most certainly can be. In class when children don't know something, they would rather not raise their hand to say they don't understand because they're worried that asking will make the other kids whisper to each other saying, "So-and-So is so dumb." This leads to our children not knowing things they should and need to know. This leads some children to act out in school, just so they can take the focus off what they don't know. In some cases, they resort to being the class clown because it's easier for them to laugh it off, rather than deal with the issue.

If we do our due diligence on what causes our children to act out, then maybe we can get to the root of the problem so that we can curb all that acting out and the "class clown" antics. But some parents are so out of touch with what's required of and from them. In parenting you have to be well balanced! You have some that are so extreme with being strict, thinking that this will solve the problem. Then you have some that try to be so cool with their children, acting more like friends, thinking this will do the trick. Not even! You have to find that middle ground and have that balance Know that, if your child doesn't know how to ask for help or want to, you share some, if not all of the blame. Communication is the key to a healthy relationship.

Therefore, speak with your children all the time, so they understand. When you don't speak in language that they understand (or even just don't speak to them enough), they won't understand. Stop thinking that they're automatically supposed to get it. Make sure they *do* get it.

My children know that we don't have any secrets in our family. This alleviates some of the problems. It avoids the possibility of someone hurting one of them and saying, "It's a secret." No. My kids are going to say, "We don't keep secrets in my family." My daughter's grandmother told my daughter at a young age, "Your privates is ya cookie jar, and if anybody ever put, they hands in your cookie jar, you come tell me!" Talking to them in their language or a way they understand helps them get it early in life. This makes it easy for them to come to you to ask for help or tell you if something happens to them.

If you're a child, don't think that you cannot help your parents. Just because sometimes the parents don't understand, doesn't mean you cannot help them understand. If you teach them the importance of asking for help, it may help or save your younger siblings from any harm in the future or from dealing with issues that come from not knowing. Each one teaches one. That's what family is for.

I was having a problem connecting with some of my children back when I had the misconception of what "fatherhood" was in my heart. So, I went to one of my older daughters and asked, "How can I have a better bond with them?" The advice she gave me was so on point. I'm in jail at the time, so all my thinking that I could buy their love and attention was gone. I had to think outside the box. Right outside the box, there was my daughter ready to help me get all the answers I needed to fix the problem and make things better. Had I not asked my child for "help", I'd still be lost trying to figure it out! That's a prime example of how and why asking for help can be so good and beneficial. Had I had too much pride or thought I knew it all, I'd still be dealing with the problem. Also, I'd have been allowing more time to go by without correcting things with my children.

Even to this day I see grown men refuse to ask for help when they know they need help with something. Some of us have too much pride. You know the saying, "...pride comes before the fall." As a man, you have to be able to admit that you don't know everything. How will the child receive proper understanding of this? He or she sees Father trying to change a flat tire on the car. Clear as day, the child can see that Dad don't know what he's doing, but because the child is watching, Dad refuses to seek help. That is how this way of thinking is passed down. If we believe it is something we should know or think we do know how to do, then we feel some type of way when it comes to asking for help. Plus, *my father didn't ask for help, so maybe I should keep going until I figure it out.* But what happens when we equate this to everything in life? It becomes widespread and second nature for us to not ask for help. Whether it's from pride, fear, or shame, we must change this misconception. If we do not, we will continue to have unnecessary suicides, mental health problems, and "wild child" kids. We'll have boys, girls, women, and men all unable to fulfill their obligations because they don't know how.

Changing this misconception requires communication as the key. We must communicate to our little ones how the wise boys and girls are the ones that first run and get the answers to the questions they don't know. We must get across how the wise one is the one who realizes he needs help. They also need to hear that when you ask for help, this makes you smarter than those that don't ask because you leave no rock unturned. Our goal must be to recondition the younger ones' minds. We must teach them that the way they thought was right is wrong. Actually, it was a misconception. How will you contribute to changing the way young people perceive asking for help? Get personal with this question. Envision your child being the one that needed help somewhere down the line but never receives it due to incorrect perceptions of asking for help. Think of your brother or sister that saw something that messed their head up a lot or experienced some sort of mistreatment that caused trauma to his or her mind and soul. Consider whether, due to him or her not knowing how to seek help to deal with it or get it to stop, the result is suicide or ruining his or her life with unhealthy activities or lifestyle. These issues should very well make you want to be more active to save someone you love.

As I thought about misconceptions when this book was first coming alive, I asked my daughter, "What are some misconceptions that people your age deal with?" She told me how the misconception of asking for help indicating that you're weak or dumb and how peer pressure is 10 times worse for her generation. She said what people think of you is at the top of the list of things that are important, so it affects young people even more now, than when I was her age. For that reason, I had to do my best to shed as much light as I could on this misconception. I had to give examples and scenarios of how and why this starts, when it starts, and all the issues linked to this misconception! I had to provide hope for changing some things we do or don't do along the way.

I'm no doctor or nothing like that, but I saw what not asking for help can do to a person. Not getting the help you need can be the difference between life and death. I saw that it's important that we keep this in mind in our dealings with our children, younger brothers, sisters, nieces, and nephews to make them feel comfortable about talking to us and asking for help. We must recondition their minds to the point that they know and understand the wise person is the one that asks for help when they need it or when they don't know something. NO ONE knows it all! NO ONE person can defeat the world. Only together do we have the power to save each other.

Hadith: "If you ask, ask Allah [God]. If you seek help, seek help from Allah [God]. Know that if all the people get together in order to benefit you with something, they will not be able to benefit you in anything except what Allah [God] has decreed for you. And if they all get together in order to harm you with something, they will not be able to harm you in anything except what Allah [God] decreed for you."

CHAPTER 8

Gambling

The misconception in gambling is thinking it's okay to take the risk, knowing you can't afford to lose! Gambling is one of the Number One ways to lose it all — Money, family, and your life! Yet I've heard countless people say, "Yeah, I gamble but I'm a winner." Sometimes I hear another common saying among gamblers, "I win more then I lose!" What? You know you're taking a risk and the chance is you can lose, yet you still will take it? Possibly you may be of those who say, "I'm in control of it," or "Whatever I lose I can afford to lose because the reward is worth the risk anyway." But what happens when you can't afford to lose? You lose what you don't have! This is what you first need to think about. It can definitely get out of control fast. I'm talking about so many different scenarios that get out of control fast: The men or women that gamble all their money and then can't even pay their rent, car payments, or even phone bills. They become subject to doing whatever they must do to get the money they need. If no one is there to give you the money you need, the next step is to do what you got to do to get the money you need because you do need it, right?

This is when we may rationalize something that's normally something we wouldn't even do, to make it doable. No more just staying in ya lane; now you got to cross over so you can get what you need by any means necessary.

Everyone gambles! I mean, everyone can be considered a gambler of some sort. Everyone has gambled a time or two, right? You don't agree? Understand something: there are so many different forms of gambling. I hope to touch on as many as I can so after you finish reading this chapter, I hope you can relate and understand how this, too, keeps us from reaching our full potential as black folks.

Let me start with inconspicuous gambling. You know the gamble that's not all that noticeable. Take, for example, the young woman who's just starting her adult life, graduated high school, is on her way to college or to work a good job. She falls for this boy she likes or even loves. Love in itself has a way of clouding our vision or judgment. Still, we gamble on it, taking the risk because the risk is worth the reward — or is it?

This woman, she's no fool. She knows this boy she loves is in the streets. Let's be real, this is a part of how she was drawn in. Good girls love bad boys, right? Little do she know, loving this boy is one of the biggest gambles ever. In her eyes she doesn't gamble at all, but he does. He's a risk taker. He lives in the moment. He does it all in the pursuit of happiness and success. He gambles!

One day, she lets him use her car while she's at work so he can do his ripping and running. She's trying to be supportive and help her boyfriend in any way she can. How many times have we seen this? Well, on this particular day that he has her car, he gets a phone call: "Yo, Bra, it's some out-of-town dudes that be hustling in my building. They gone right now. I know it's close to $100,000 in they spot! Easy lick for you, Bro'." It don't take long at all for the boyfriend to make up his mind that this is a blessing. He pulls off the home invasion real easy. He's in and out in no time. On his way out, he jumps in the car and skirts off a little too wild, just as the out-of-town dudes are pulling up! His girl's car is a unique-colored car that the dudes look at. Something seems a little off to them. Sure enough, when they go in their spot, it's clear that they have just been robbed. It doesn't take a rocket scientist to know whoever was in that car had to be responsible.

Two days later as fate would have it, the out-of-town dudes see the same car that skirted off from their building the day of the robbery. As boyfriend is picking up his girl from work, the out-of-town guys spot him as the same car from the day they were robbed so they follow the car for a few blocks. Then, at the stop light and no questions asked, they pull up on the driver's side door and squeeze 12 shots into the car. Dude in the car lived, but his lady was dead before her head hit the steering wheel.

Sad story, but it's a true-to-life story. Innocent people lose their lives all the time because of someone else's gamble. You lose when they gamble, and you don't even gamble, per se. That's the inconspicuous gamble. It's when you don't fully know the person you choose to let enter your life. You, too, are a gambler. This is a lesson for my young ladies.

"My auntie got AIDS and I'm watching her suffer. Why she gotta die because she was in love with a hustler." - Plies, from "Family Straight" on the 2008 album, *DARealist*.

Gambling is always a risk, a chance taken. Sometimes there's no reward and only ruin. Over the years, the next gamble's negative statistics have shot through the roof. It really affects us and our families and threatens our future existence more then we care to realize. I'm talking about the gamble of unprotected sex and what it can bring you and lead to. "The shit was so sloppy I had to roll the dice..." (Migos' 2017 single and video, "Too Hotty") This line refers to a woman's vagina being so wet and for that reason alone I had to gamble. It's just so simple that it's compared to something as simple as rolling dice. We might hear this song, this line, and say, "Yeah, me too," because we can relate. We think, this shit is cool; it's cool to gamble and take this risk. Everybody we grew up around made it look cool and does it. Nothing being wrong with this picture! It's so cool that we brag to our friends, "Yeah, I had sex with girly last night, raw [without condom]!" You may have a friend say about the girl, "You know she fuck everybody," and you say, "Yeah, I know, but I had to. I couldn't help it. I had to feel it." It's not just the fellas either, the females be on the same type of time. I can't tell you all the female reasons for letting a man go in them without a condom, but I would imagine some saying, "I'm trying to have his baby," or "We would make a cute baby," or "I love him so much. If I get pregnant then I got him for life."

All these reasons show the ignorance in us. It shows our disregard for life, for health. Temporary pleasure you feel or just want to feel can cause you a lifetime of pain. Isn't that too much of a risk for only what — a few minutes of pleasure, sometimes?

Death is real. AIDS is real! Herpes is real! All the host of other sexually transmitted diseases are real. Then why is it so common for us to gamble with our life so easily? (I say "us" because I, too, was guilty of these thoughts and feelings so, if anybody understands, I definitely understand.) I was so caught up living in the moment, not even thinking about my tomorrows, so if you thinking like that too, then you're not thinking right. I get it, the drugs cloud our judgment big time; our circumstances cloud our judgment as well. But if you're sitting in a jail cell like I am right now, without the drugs to cloud your judgment and no longer running from things, then when you think about what's being said? You got to be like, "Damn, I was tripping!"

It's okay to admit when you're wrong. It's okay to want to recondition your mind. It's okay to want to live a nice long life. It's okay to hit the restart button and start all over. Change your thinking. Dare to be different. Dare to be a leader. Dare to live and make your mother and father proud. If you have children, make them proud. Be there for them, this is what you're supposed to do.

Understand that those people that you grew up around that made it look cool and sound cool to have unprotected sex are the losers that may not be around to see their kids or family grow up. Know that they are the clowns and you no longer laugh with them. You're laughing at them because they just don't get it.

These are the ones that, after you tell them, "Yo! You are gambling with ya life having sex with that person unprotected," they will say to you, "It was worth the gamble because it was good." They be the ones that tell you, "It had a little smell, but it was still good." Do we not know what the smell implies? Possible danger! You got to know that this type of person has a serious disregard for life! Do you have a daughter? Do you have a son? Do you want this type of behavior passed down to them? If we don't change the narrative, then this is how they will keep being taught. Do you want to teach them the correct way? Or do you want them to be misled by the same misconceptions as you were?

Times are ten times worse now than when I was a teenager. Back then, you could have unprotected sex and have a 90% chance of walking out of there unharmed! What is it now, a 50-50% chance? This is how bad the times have gotten with diseases and things, and that the age has become so early that our people meet these problems. Do our misconceptions have something to do with it?

The type of guy or girl you involve yourself with is also a gamble if you don't know the person. Because he or she could go out and have unprotected sex with someone, get something, and bring it back to you.

You are much better off if you don't shoot dice, bet on sporting events, or even go to the casino and say you don't gamble. But if you have unprotected sex. know that you may do the most severe gambling of all.

When you join a gang you also are gambling with ya life and freedom. It's only a chance you make it to your next birthday! Beefs with the other side of town or other gangs are deadly! Think about how it would feel if you died as a result of these gang beefs. Let's say it's one or two years later and those two gangs are now the best of friends. I mean they hang out together and the whole nine. What did you die for? Nothing at all! You died in vain. How will that feel? Oh, you won't be feeling nothing in this life because you won't be here no more. The rest of the homies are here living they best life, getting married, sitting among each other saying, "This beef shit is stupid; it got to be about getting money and getting ahead, not beefing with each other." But when you were alive, ya position was the lyrics …pistol in ya pants in ya stance like fuck you, I'm from the other side where we ride like a bus do…" (Rick Ross' "White House" track #12, 2008 album *Port of Miami*) This is how they taught you to feel and think. This is one of them times you take yaself out of ya body ahead of time so you can imagine losing ya life. You can think about the possibility of the gamble you're taking and how it can cost you ya life. Do you want to live or die? To me this is one of the more senseless gambles!

Now, this one right here, by far was my favorite gamble: HUSTLING, selling drugs, to be exact! You couldn't tell me I wasn't born to sell drugs. To make matters worse, I loved it. I loved how it made things "better" for me. I thought I could do it forever. Who was going to stop me from doing it? Who was going to get in the way of the feeling it brought forth for me? I was scammed by the feeling of security it brought on, the feeling of being able to be a provider, the feeling of being "Da Man".

Early on, you could never convince me that selling drugs was a risk or gamble. To so many of us it was a means of survival. Live or die, eat or you starve, when you're living in the moment, you're not thinking about the worse that could happen. You may start off in survival mode, and that quickly changes. It advances to, "I can win at this game. I can gamble and really win big." I thought, *This shit is easy, I seen dudes downfall and all I have to do is stay focused, pay attention, stick to the script, stay out the way, and don't be too greedy.*

But things rarely go according to plan without a lot of bumps in the road or worse, you falling into a ditch. You do know what a ditch is, right? You can look at it as a grave, no coming back from that. All for a means of a survival, a meal, or even a "mil"? Let's be real, how many millionaire drug dealers do we really know? Alright, how many "hundred-thousandaires" do we know? Now ask yaself, "How many men and women do we know in jail from pursuing these drug-dealer-kingpin dreams of coming all the way up? How many have been sentenced more years than they can even live, for crimes that don't even fit the time? And it was all in the pursuit of getting ahead, of taking that gamble! About twenty-five years ago, I remember my mother saying, "You must not be that good at it, you always get caught."

She killed me with that line. Instead of taking the wisdom from her words and just admitting that she was right, my pride and arrogance made me say back to her, "If I hustle all year long and get caught one day, that doesn't mean I always get caught!" Mom dukes wasn't about to go back and forth with me, she just gave me that look. It said, "Whatever," but her eyes also said *you going to learn the hard way, I see!* My ignorant ass felt like I had all the sense and all the answers. Plus, I felt like I had so much invested in getting ahead by means of selling drugs because I had tunnel vision. I was a man now, so I could gamble if wanted to. I could handle whatever came with it — or could I?

This is where ignorance prevails. "Niggas think of quarter keys and scales when they mention me, graveyards and penitentiary bars, I told 'em sign me up…" (Jeezy, lyrics from "Spyder", track 1 on his album, *Pressure*) Jeezy is my guy, let's not get that misconstrued, but when you listen to these rap songs, you have to be able to hear and understand the references. The metaphor being used here is: "…when you mention my name…" you think of a hustler, no doubt about it. But the "graveyard and penitentiary bars, I told 'em sign me up…" means you have to know that's the gamble you take when selling drugs. It may sound cool but it's not cool. You have to be able to hear and understand the figure of speech: Sign me up for jail or death? Who in they right mind signs up to go to jail or die? It's putting emphasis on the risk involved in hustling, the ultimate gamble. Besides these could have been Jeezy's thoughts *before* he found his way out. Once his worth was more than $20,000 dollars a show, know that he wasn't saying then: sign me up for jail or death! It's ya job to find your way out! Find your way to success.

In no way am I trying to preach, that is not what this is about. This is more about sharing the experience and downfalls of me and millions of boys and men like me who share these same thoughts and feelings. It's about me looking for how I can be some help when it comes to a better way of thinking. Better ways and new ideas are our goal!

I don't remember who said it to me, but I remember what was

said to me: "If you put the same energy that you put into selling drugs into something else, you're going to be rich." You should know that the probability of your success being a drug dealer is very slim. The gamble is so stacked against you. You have to avoid the cops, the robbers, and then you also have to avoid your friends. You know, the jealous ones that feel like they should have more than you or have the girl you're with. These "frenemies" also don't forget about the extra girlfriends that can't take being your side piece no more, the ones you only play with sometimes, or when you need to use them. Well, be aware that sometimes leads to them giving you up to the robbers or cops one day. Yes. Being a drug dealer, a successful drug dealer, means the odds are already stacked against you! It's a gamble that you'll more than likely lose at some point.

Oh, and don't forget to factor in how you could get 20-30 years for "ghost drugs". Those are drugs that don't even exist or wasn't even present on the scene. Maybe it's just having two or three people saying you sold them drugs before. They can be lying or just trying to get their own self out of a jam. If this isn't a gamble, then I don't know what is.

So, hear me: even if it started out as survival or to feed yourself or even just to get by or if you felt like you didn't have a choice, hustling drugs could very well lead to your demise, as well as your exit out of this world. I don't know about you, but I want a chance to win, not a probability to lose or become a statistic. That's what we become when we gamble this way.

To put this all together, the misconception that gambling is not a big deal can be a very dangerous way of thinking on a lot of different cylinders. As far as freedom goes, ask yourself if it's really worth giving up so many years of your life to jail when you only get a certain number of years to live? So many of us spend more than half our life in jail and never really get a chance to live. My *old* head use to say about guys that keep coming back and forth to jail, "He's doing life in jail in installments. One of these times he's going to come and be stuck like me, never able to get out." That is so likely to happen because we look at gambling as not being a big deal.

To the guy who likes to gamble with the ladies and the ladies that like to gamble with the guys. I know you want no strings attached, just want to have a little fun, just want to live. Then do that then, LIVE. Know that the "fun" is a gamble because out of all the guys and girls you run into, everybody has secrets and untold truths! They may have something that you really don't want. Sex without the condom is a gamble. Don't look at it as not being a big deal. To me, dealing with someone that you don't fully know is one of the stupidest gambles ever, because you don't know what you're up against! All types of dangers could be right around the corner because of what someone else is into. You think you don't even gamble. You think you're doing everything right in your life. Yet you're going to allow someone else to ruin your hopes, goals, and dreams because they don't have none? For my young ladies, that's just something to always be aware of! Being aware is how to be alive.

I hope and pray I can open up someone's eyes to how we live and gamble, consciously and unconsciously. With the idea that we can look at things a little differently, I hope you see how it effects our life directly and indirectly. I write this with hopes of educating each other (our sisters, brothers, and our children) about gambling in every form possible. Don't gamble something that means something to you! Don't gamble something you cannot get back! Don't be fooled by these misconceptions and don't gamble what you cannot afford to lose!!!

CHAPTER 9

Women Raising Men

Now comes the misconception that women can't raise a man! What about when a woman doesn't have a choice, when the father refuses to raise his son? What about when the father's fate is death, because we all have to go someday and some a lot sooner than others. What about in the times of war when dad has to go fight in the war? What about when dad makes a mistake in life and has to pay for his actions and goes to jail for a long period of time? There are several instances when a woman doesn't have a choice. So, what is she to do? Should she give up because she's a man short? Absolutely not! Like I mentioned before, some of the most underappreciated people in the world are our women. They been doing this since the beginning of time. Who says they can't raise a man? But believe it or not, a lot of women succumb to this misconception! They begin to believe it and will find every excuse to further say they "can't raise a man."

Ladies, women! Do not find a reason to say you cannot raise a man. Find a reason why you can! I've seen women put their sons out way too soon. Now, it does come a time when enough is just enough, but don't let that be your excuse too soon. Stick in there and fight a little longer. Remember NO ONE will love this boy, this future man the way you will. There's no stronger bond of love than a mother has for her son. He may need just a bit more of your love and support, especially if the father is non-existing. Please, don't let that resentment toward the child's father become resentment of your son. His father may have deceived you, lied to you, broke your heart, and even left you and your son for dead. As he grows, your son is looking more and more like his father and acting like him. Lot of times this can recreate the original hurt and pain. Still, don't be bitter, be better!

Your hard work will pay off! Your prayers and faith will pay off! Someone once said, "A mother's prayer for her child will be heard and answered if you truly believe." The reminder benefits the believer!

For this reason, I say to all the mothers of the world: "Continue to fight. Continue to teach our boys. We will eventually hear everything you say to us!" It took me over 30 years to begin to understand my mother's teachings, love, and guidance. In that time, she never gave up on me. After I was grown, she continued to raise her son to be a man with sound advice, love, and guidance. So, ladies, don't give up. Some of us take longer than others to get it, but better late than never! Just don't give up because, most times, ya'll are all we got.

"The only boy our women cannot raise to be a man, is a boy who thinks he's already a man."

CHAPTER 10

Love

Time to speak of the misconceptions about love. Believe it or not this was a last-minute decision for me to try to enlighten you on misconceptions about love. Who am I to speak on love? I am a man that obviously had it all wrong too! Then, why wouldn't I speak on love? Who better to get it from? You could learn from my mistakes and wrong way of seeing love! It would have been truly a disservice to not speak about this particular subject because we need a little more of this in the world today.

Love has got to be one of the most misused and misplaced words ever to be spoken! I don't mean misused just by men, or by a particular race, or even by women I mean misused by everyone!

We interpret this word "love" incorrectly all day every day. We equate love to "like" all the time. We equate love to lust just as much. We use this word to get what we want. We use this word to put someone at ease. We also use his word to deceive. The word love rolls off your tongue so effortlessly. It rolls so much that you begin to believe that you do love this person or that you refer to.

When we speak of the misconception about love, we speak of it as being love in error, love being false, love being an illusion, love being a myth, love being untrue, and love not being fulfilled!

Let's be clear as to misconceptions about love and what that means. I'm going to break this down in a way that may never have been broken down to you before. Afterwards, it will be up to you to take a real good look in the mirror and ask yourself: *did I really love her, him, them, or it the way I was supposed to?*

The first person I need to address is myself and those like me. I'm talking to the ones who "loved" the streets. How do you love something that will never love you back? How do you risk your life for something that is false? How do you "love" something that will give itself to any stranger that comes along, something that will never be yours? That is not love. That is an illusion, for sure!

Maybe I wasn't that naive. Maybe it wasn't the streets I "loved". Maybe it was the couple dollars I made in the streets? Maybe it was the attention I got? maybe it was my homeboys? Maybe it was the girls? Maybe it was the sense of feeling like I belonged? Maybe it was all those things and more that led me to believe I "loved" the streets! But truth be told, love doesn't bring forth so much pain!

Love is a strong affection, a warm attachment, fondness, cherishing, prizing, treasuring, valuing, respecting, adoring, worshiping, idolizing someone or something, just to name a few of its traits. None of these words equal or amount to the word pain. Surely, you got to know and understand you're sure to feel some type of pain "loving" the streets.

I lost my brother to the streets! I lost every dollar I made! The attention was gone! My homeboys was gone and the girls was gone! After giving so much of me, so much of my care and attention (love) to the streets, I had NOTHING to show for me "loving" them so much, well, nothing but a long prison sentence! Maybe I'm one of the lucky ones, though. So many more lose all that and more — they lose their life!

I had to start with this harsh reality first to show there is a heavy price to pay for my misconceptions. I need my readers to know about the heavy burden of waking up every day knowing that you're not going home for a long time. I said it before, and I will say it again: in jail, you sometimes dread waking up from your dreams! In no way do you desire to die, but you do awake from your dreams just to realize you're in jail and you're not getting out for a long time, or never! You most certainly feel some regret about your actions and misplaced "love"!

Again, I had to lead off with the streets because every "love" I discovered after this false love of the streets somehow tainted my perception and understanding of what love really is. It changed everything that I think I love, or could love, because I developed my misconception of what love is so early in life.

Due to my misconceptions of love, every event, thing, and person that required my love was not given my love correctly. Even though you and I might have recognized some of the other misconceptions in this book before the misconception of love, I still believe this is the most profound one of them all.

Love is required in so much of our daily life! Love is required in our relationship with our children. Love is required in our relationship with our parents. Love is required in our relationship with our wife or girlfriend, husband, or boyfriend. It is required for our siblings, friends, careers, lives, ourselves, and most importantly, the One who created us. Whoever you refer to as your Creator, you must love and be able to display love for that One. But how do you display love, if your perception of love is wrong, if it is incorrect?

I know you hear people all the time say, "I love my child," "I love my children," or "I love them more than anything in this world." You hear them say that and then go right outside to sell drugs or rob someone. You got women that will also do their things that run the same risk as the men. They don't love their child correctly, because if they did, they wouldn't be doing anything to jeopardize being there for the child that's going to need its parents. I'm not going to be so harsh to say they don't love them at all. I will say that, at the time they take the risk, they aren't loving their children in that moment. On the other hand, it might be fair to say they loved doing whatever they were doing more than they loved their children.

Some will even try to excuse their actions by saying, "I do what I do *because* I do love my child." Others say things like, "I'm a man, so it's my duty to make a way out of no way if I have to for my children, by any means necessary, right?" Wrong! That's the misconception of what love is that's like I'm talking about. What we heard and seen and took at face value to be true was wrong! Providing is only a part of your duty! Your main duty or purpose is to be there and to not do anything to take yaself away from your kids. Remember, this misconception also means something goes unfulfilled. When you love correctly, you have to fulfill all aspects of that love in order for saying you love to be a true statement. "I love my children," you say — but do you really?

The same applies to your love for a girlfriend, wife, boyfriend, or husband. Sometimes we think we're "in love" or we "love" someone and we're not even close to doing it. Sometimes we think that because the sex is good, we love this or that person. Oftentimes, because a person gives us things, gifts, money, or pays some bills it means he or she must love me. We think, "I love her because of what she does for me." That's just it, you love what the person does, you don't love him or her. If you take away the great sex, do you still love her? If you take away the money, gifts, and security, do you still love him? Sometimes you still will love that person. But most times you won't, because most times, the love was based on the wrong thing! It was based on what drew us in, what attracted us the most. Once we're able to capture that, we felt like it had to be love we were feeling since we didn't actually know if it really was love.

This misconception isn't just applied to the one who thinks he's giving the love, it's also with the ones who believe they're receiving the love. Think of the misconception that you can cheat on the one you claim to "love", and still believe you love them. It applies also to the one that gets cheated on who, in spite of the mistreatment, thinks the cheating person loves them. This has become so normal to our perception of what love is. Well, love isn't supposed to hurt. Love is the opposite of hurt. I don't know about you, but I don't want my daughters to have to experience the hurt and pain that's become so common in relationships today. Therefore, it's our job to educate our little girls and boys on the correct way to love in order to change today's misconception of love and stop it from continuing to be passed on to our future generations. It has to stop, reset, and restart somewhere. Why not have it corrected with you and yours coming in the future?

To doing that, first one must drive it home with their children to know that they must love themselves before they can love someone else. They must know and understand that if they love themselves, they won't ever allow someone to mistreat them or cheat on them or put hands on them because none of that equals love. We must teach children all the signs of what love is, as well as what love isn't! They must know that some people they may want to love or like aren't even capable of loving them. Whether it's because those folks never felt love or whether it's because they don't even love themselves, children must know to ask themselves: how would that person be able to love me? Of course, some people just may not be ready to love yet. In other cases, the person they like only loves himself with no intentions of loving your daughter. Yes, I get personal with this thing we call love, because who better to teach your daughter than the one who was that little boy at one point? When the raw truth is spoken, is taught the correct way, it paves the way so our children will not be blind or naïve. Knowing is half the battle. I'd love for my daughters to be able to tell a boy who has a girlfriend already, "No thank you, my father warned me about the signs of a boy who displays characteristics of someone with a misconception of what love is." My daughters will know if he treats or cheats other girls like that then it's a good chance this is who he is. When someone shows you who they are, believe them.

Some of us are so in love with the thought of being "in love", that we will jump right into something with the hopes of being able to get and give real love. The hell with that goofy shit. You love when someone is deserving of your love! On top of that, you cannot love and receive love until you interpret love correctly.

I've heard women and girls make comments regarding being cheated on. They said, "He cheated but I know he loves me." I heard some say, "Them other girls want him, but I got him." Do you really, now? You probably don't! He don't love you. Or at least it's safe to say that when he's with the other woman, he's not loving you! Therefore, you have to love yourself! Know your worth! Don't love any man or woman more than you love yaself! In this scenario, both sides have the same misconception of what love is.

I know a couple of young boys reading this may be saying "Fareed, you sounding like a player hater." That's not the case at all. The case is that Fareed has five beautiful daughters and I need them to know the real! You know "keeping it real", right? Well, this is keeping it real with the most important beings walking this earth, our daughters! Not that I love them more then I love my boys, but little girls require a little more protecting, loving, and teaching because boys are naturally stronger than girls! As a father, I believe our Number One job is to protect and love our princesses the correct way. When you have a daughter it changes you, and changes how you see things! You wouldn't want nobody cheating on your daughter, or putting their hands on ya daughter and passing it off as love, right? I guess I'm not saying nothing wrong after all.

Again, I'm talking from firsthand experience and mistakes, so I be knowing too, I'm still a little hip. Looking at how I was so-called "loving" my girlfriends in the past, I realize I didn't see all the wrong in my actions. Society, movies, and my environment told us and showed us we could have a main girl and a few side girls. I saw, so I learned that as long as we did a little more for the main girl, that meant we loved her, and she stood ahead of the rest. It was accepted as being love, but really was just another misconception: love unfulfilled.

Here's another misconception we have with loving our children. As parents, we tend to let our children do what they want. Because we love them, we want to give them freedom, allow them to have fun, make their own decisions, choose their own friends. A lot of times we do this in attempts to get them to love us more, especially if we've fallen short in giving our love to them! This is the misconception I call love in error. No. Love is sometimes having to make the tough choices, the hard decisions because we are more mature! "I cannot let you be friends with someone I know will bring you down or turn you on to things a child is not supposed to be involved in. I love you, so I will not let you be friends with them. I will choose your friends for you because I love you and I know better. So, if you cannot find positive, good friends then I will find good friends for you!" When we love correctly, we will guide their decisions. We will give them a little freedom but not too much! I've heard kids say, "My parents love me. They let me do whatever I want to do." It's just another way love is misconceived by both the parent that allows it, and the kid that's allowed to do whatever.

Again, that love is unfulfilled!

What gave me a better understanding of love and what it truly means? I believe a lot of it had to do with me being in jail and not getting love from some people that I figured would always love me. Next, I was getting love from someone that loved me when loving me was hard as hell! That is when I really started to reflect on what she was doing for me when she didn't have to and I thought, why? Then it became so clear. She did it because she *loved* me! I couldn't rub her feet. I couldn't pay a bill. I couldn't have sex with her! Still, she went on this journey with me, loving me every step of the way. Her love wasn't in error. It wasn't false, an illusion, a myth, untrue, or unfulfilled. It was REAL! Her pure love for me made me look in the mirror and ask myself: "Did I ever love anyone or anything this way?" The answer was no. And it was because I didn't know the correct meaning of love! I never loved any woman the correct way prior to her! I didn't love my children the correct way! I didn't even love myself! This woman helped teach me the true meaning of love! Her love allowed me to examine myself as well as my love, or what I thought love was, in order to correct it. Her love allowed me to make changes so that I could give that correct love to my children, to my parents and most importantly, to the Creator of the heavens and the earth!

Through my trials and tribulations, even family members left me for dead, never visited, never sent a letter, a picture, or a penny. That made me feel like it was no love from them, yet she would never speak ill about them! I'm thinking she would take my side and be like, "Yeah fuck them, they dis my bay." But she would just say, "Love them from a distance." Here I am hurt, and she still pushes for me to love them.

Of course, she would also say, "What you complaining about, lack of love? Boy, please, you're winning. You got me!" In no way am I saying she made me, but she made me *think*! My mother always told me I needed a woman who helped bring out the best in me. Well, I got that now, Mom, and because of her I'm no longer misled by my misconceptions of love.

I can now say: "The best experience of life is Love!

Grandma Tiny

Grandpa McClure, Mum-Mum, (GrandMom) My Mother, Arlean

Me and Rasheeta

My Mother & Me

My Mother, Me, Laicie, Tariq

Tyson 2016

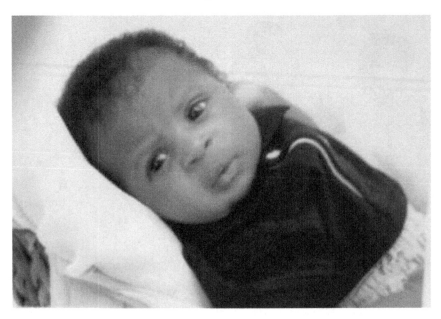

Eid Feast "2019"
Lil Bro Daquan & Fareed

CHAPTER 11

Being a Gangster or Thug Part 2, by Keith McCrory

My name is "Keith Cash", as the hood would call me. I would like to give you my timeless journey, hopefully to convey beneficial bits and pieces as to who I am. This is who I have been for 53 years on this planet, dealing with my misconceptions.

First, I must thank a man, an author, and my comrade for even allowing me to add to his life's work. Much respect, Fareed.

I begin with saying I am a known risk-taker and I know the biggest risk is not taking any! The past is our definition. We may strive, with good reason, to escape it or to escape what is bad in it. However, I realize we will escape it only by adding something better to our life. For reasons I haven't figured out yet, I chose to sell drugs. I did that since the age of 12 years old, until my incarceration 3 years ago. So, for 38 years of my life I have lived with the misconception of being a gangster, a drug dealer!

I have always heard the saying that "time changes things", but I now know you actually have to change yourself. It took me 50-something years to realize my "net worth" to the world is usually determined by what remains after your bad habits are subtracted from your good ones. I must admit, I just recently started thinking about this almighty question my guy Fareed posed to me. He asked me, "When was enough enough for you?" Shame on me! I'm going to be totally honest with my guy, Fareed, and his readership. It was never a serious thought until Feb. 12, 2017. Why? That day happens to be the day I was arrested at my children's school. I know. Wow, right? I'm just glad my kids didn't witness my arrest. It was a wakeup call for me, for real. In short, I received a 37-month federal bid or sentence. It happens to be my second federal bid, the first being a 20-year sentence.

It took me 53 years of my life to realize that the bureaucracy is catching up with the industry of drug dealing. As I saw it, for most of my life, people like myself, the so-called gangsters, wasn't afraid of the true gangsters, the Feds! The gangster in me thought I was too smart for them dirty feds. (Stupid ass me, LOL!) Now I believe that my thinking that way is why the government is singling out and punishing us so-called gangsters and thugs. I might add, it's at an alarming rate, too, and I believe that's to keep everyone else who think they're gangsters in line. Right now, the Feds are killing us alive, as I like to say. They're giving out football numbers (double-digit sentences) to men and women, not even thinking twice about it. For sure, it also has become clear to me that it is only a matter of time before "the chickens come home to roost" since the government is doing whatever it can to catch the gangsters and thugs. The industry of drug dealing is a fading industry in my eyes. These days, you play ball with the government or you're screwed. Believe me, most so-called gangsters and thugs are almost all *too* willing to play softball with the government.

Keep this in mind, a creative adult is a child who survives. I am no longer a child, so I decided to use my adult mindset. I decided that, after spending this time away from my family and friends, I will not grant the government an all-access pass to my life. I do understand that unacceptable treatment is sometimes essential to spark our genius. But now I say, "Enough is enough!"

I now take pride in saying I choose family over this industry of the drug game. Today April 9th, 2020. You ask me why? Because a good friend of mine posed that million-dollar question to me about a week ago. From the day my comrade, Fareed, asked me the question, I've done nothing but put super thought into the question. I also want to say on record that I've been asked this question three or four times and never had an answer either time. So, I say thank you to my brother Fareed for pushing me to do what is right for me and my family. Love is love, fam.

I am ready to venture towards my new life. If you never venture, you never gain. Being that dynamic man, I will proceed along the path of knowledge and rediscover the great beauty that the rest of my life has to offer me. My family and friends deserve to know the authentic "Keith Cash" and from here on out, it is going to be quality over quantity. For me it will be a much slower pace that will convey an unparalleled quality of life. I will take personal pleasure in my new journey, in which exclusivity is going to be my undeniable value. I plan to be the man who loves to choose and who seeks a unique thought process.

Even standing still, the new Keith will stand apart from the old "Keith". I now know and do believe that the only limit to my impact is my imagination and commitment to excellence. With each day I spend in prison, the picture becomes clearer to me as to where my life should be headed. I say, "What is time?" I believe it's measuring one's day, measuring one's steps, measuring one's life. I believe it's an idea that holds everyone accountable for the way we fill our days. One thing I will tell you, Fareed, I plan to waste time no longer. At the end of the day, I believe time to be one of the single, most valuable concepts ever to be created. You, Fareed, actually helped me make a decision to better utilize my time. Thank you!

Reinvention must be realized! Synergy is my new guiding purpose. Intuitive mindset is my result. I introduce to you, Fareed and your readership, the extremely new Keith Cash 2020, a new version with 99.99% of my new body stronger, lighter, faster, and laser focused. My new body is built on mind elevation that started with me discovering my actual true self!

Fareed, what I will tell you today April 9, 2020, is that I, Keith Cash know that enough is enough for your boy. I've learned to talk less, to press my ears to the pulse and listen to both friends and foes. Feeling unshakeable, I can embrace life's hard knocks by learning to bend and enhance, but above all, to follow my compass of truth, my purpose. I took the time to realize I have a great mind. I know great minds will always have purpose, while average minds just have wishes.

Before I go any further, I just hope and pray that you, too, have figured out when enough is enough for yourself. I am so looking forward to one day reading your life's work. Can't wait to hear and better yet, read about it when you figure it out. Time for us good guys to be gangster at something other than gangsters, drug dealers, and thugs. We can take up being gangster dads, gangster husbands, gangster sons, and gangster friends. At least we can still keep the gangster part (LMAO). Yeah. I say let's be as gangster as we can be the right way this time around. My friend, we got this.

I also want to thank you for the pure unadulterated conversation that we shared during our time together. I want the world to know that it was always a pleasure and refreshing when we spoke together. Your readership needs to know that Mr. Fareed is a wonderful human being to be around. Given the circumstances of how we met in prison, this is saying a lot. For the readers who haven't been to prison, it is not the highest quality of men in there.

So, when you run across a quality guy, you take notice. Another little fact is that prison is so segregated nowadays. Fareed is from Pennsylvania and I am from New York. People from the two states sometimes don't get along. But Fareed and I are two older men who recognize real men. We have a saying inside that goes, "Men (at least real men) attract and boys attack."

Life is woven by what happens to you by chance, but also what we weave from those happenings and the patterns you create. Sure, our choices of the available options play a part as well. Those options expand and change each time you make a new choice to set your life on a new path. You must always stay adaptable. You now know you have to develop the muscles in form of sustainable behavior that enables you to quickly recognize and adapt to change on the fly.

Yo, Fareed. I just want to say how proud and honored I am to have met you. I wish you nothing but the best with your venture, your new life and career goals. I know you will achieve true greatness from this day forth. Now, hurry up and get me my signed copy of your life work on paper. Do I predict best seller list? Now, why wouldn't I? Keep doing what you're doing Brother, you're an inspiration to enough people that will turn into many more. Fareed, when we speak, I can see in your eyes that you're determined to overcome all odds to achieve the ultimate goal as you define success. I am witnessing you get in touch with your own potential in a metaphysical way. I have learned that when you feel you have given it your all, you're prepared to say, "That is it. I'm done," But guys like us know that there's always something more, some hidden energy inside your body or mind, that you can find more to achieve if you are curious enough.

I can't say it enough. Thank you for being that guy who woke me up to be my new best me. Your question was just that powerful. Mr. Fareed, I can just imagine how many other men, women, boys, and girls your book is going to impact. Stay being real and you will go on to do fantastic things.

CHAPTER 12

Being a Gangster Is Cool Part 3 by Turone Bason (Beans)

Fareed! As-salamu alaikum, Big Bro'. Thanks for giving me the opportunity to be a part of your first book. I appreciate it and wish you the best.

My name is Turone Bason, but everybody knows me as "Beans". I'm currently at FCI Schuylkill serving a 60-month federal bid, a sentence for a gun charge. I'm from the dirty streets of Mt. Vernon, NY, where I was taught, "Isn't no such thing as half-way crooks," and "Boys do what they're told; gangstas do what they want," and all that other stupid shit. I'll explain why it's stupid in a second.

January 2019, I got called back to the case manager's office to sign my half-way house papers, which allow you to go home six months early. I declined the half-way house offer and told her I would wait on my projected release date instead. The case manager looked at me like I was crazy. However, I really thought I had good reason to deny it. Besides, I still had the "boy's do what they're told and gangstas do what they want" mindset that my old heads taught me. I wanted to be able to come and go as I pleased, to forget them curfews and being bunked up with another dude in the half-way house. I'm 25 years old, I'm single, I'm dating, I may get a late-night call from my lady friend and wanna have a "date night" rendezvous. I can't go if I'm in the half-way house. My guys might be going out or something and I'm stuck in the half-way house talking about what we going to do when they let us outside tomorrow. Nah, I'm a "gangsta". I'm going to do whatever I want to do when I want to do it! This is one of the most ignorant reasons ever to not be free with my family. As I write this, I'm very disappointed in myself.

In May 2020, the coronavirus, aka COVID 19, is in full swing in New York. I got an email and my mother told me one of my favorite uncles passed away from cancer. I got in the shower and cried like a baby. When someone close to you dies, you feel it like, "This shit is real. We not going to be here forever." The following week, that uncle's brother passed of COVID. My family was just taking "L" after "L", meaning loss after loss. Yet here I am in the Feds with this ignorant, gangsta mindset, and I'm crying in the shower and shit. Can't even help my family by being there for them when I could have! I can't hug my mother and tell her everything going to be alright. I can't assist my family in any fashion because I still want to be a gangsta.

Around the time I declined the half-way house, I had a celly named Leem, from West Philly. He had 35 years to do. The cell was his, yet he welcomed me with open arms. I told him about declining the half-way house and why. He said, "That's the dumbest shit I ever heard!" He kept going saying, "You don't know what tomorrow holds for any of us. What about your family? What about your mother, your loved ones?" He continued, "Man, I got 35 years. Any chance I get, I'll run for the door." I was sitting there with the stupid face, like: *Damn! My mom is getting up there in age, my family do need me.* I shook it off and said, "They going to be alright." How selfish of me! This stupid-ass decision, based on my perception and misconception, cost me big time. In hindsight, I know we always can look back and see what we could have done different, but I was right there at freedom's door. I could have been there before my folks left this world. This is a regret I'll have to live with for the rest of my life. I'll always know how I allowed myself to be misled and believe what I did was cool and thorough.

Being a gangsta is not what it's cracked up to be. All the real gangstas are dead or in jail. The ones in jail wish they wasn't gangstas no more once they get that crazy type of time. I done walked the yard with the best of them; some of them don't got football number (a long sentence), others got letters (life)!

Truth be told, if I could rewind the hands of time, I would have taken my ass to the half-way house, so that I would have been there to support my family. I look back at it like, "Damn! I wish I wasn't trying to be a gangsta!"

CHAPTER 13

Women Raising Men Part 2 by Jamar Williams (Gorrock)

Fareed, you got a lot of good topics in your content. I'm loving what you're trying to do, Bro'. We have to do things like this because our younger generation is lost out there in the world. They need men like yourself and me to lead them in the right direction, since we've seen what wrong does. So, it's an honor that you allowed me to be able to drop some knowledge into your book. Thanks, Bro'! Peace!

Many of us have the idea in our brain that women raising men is not possible. Many of us have this idea that it takes a male figure to raise the male child into a man. If we ever have paid attention to African American history, it shows and tells us that this idea, the very thought of it, is misleading. It's true that if a male figure was in more African American households, our society would be better than it is today. However, due to inequality, oppression, mass incarceration, and racial profiling of men of color, that reality is fragile.

Let's go back to where it all started, slavery! When the so-called "master" would strip us men of not just clothes and belongings and family, but also of all our sense of responsibility, our only obligation became servitude. We were taken away from our wives and children and mentally and physically destroyed. If not killed, we would be sold off. That left the mothers to become predominant parental figures within the slave unit to raise boys to men.

This situation continued when slavery was so-called abolished. The 13th amendment did not abolish slavery. It's reconstituted slavery, instead by putting it on another plane. At some point we have to call prison exactly what it is: a perpetuation of slavery. Do we know what perpetuation of slavery means? Perpetuation means **never ending**! They don't want us to get better; they want to always have their foot on our necks. The 13th amendment says, "...neither slavery nor involuntary servitude shall exist on these lands..." Oh, but it goes on, "...except for persons duly convicted of a crime..." It is a system like this that gives judges, legislators, and politicians a vested interest in passing the laws, regulations, decisions, and judgements that keep people of color in prison. Justice cannot exist when the people in charge of defending the rights of the people are the same ones invested in their incarceration.

When dealing with a monster of this caliber, sometimes women have no choice but to raise boys to men. Are there any other no-choice situations forcing women to raise the boys? Yes, there are. The father could have passed away from a car accident, disease, or something like that and in these situations a woman has no choice. Other times, the dad is just a "dead beat", he just refuses to be a part of the boy's life. We have a lot of that too. Still, the main reason is as I stated in the beginning. The system was designed for our women to be left alone. It's up to us to change what was designed to perpetuate our downfall. But until we, as men, become conscious of what's going on in the world, the systems that hold us back, we will continue to leave our women no choice but to do our job. I salute all the women raising boys to be men. I say to all the women, "If you're already ready, then you don't have to get ready!"

Here is something to think about. If men of color make up 67% of the prison populations, who is it that's stepping up to the plate to raise our boys? It damn sure is not your homeboys! Who is it that's giving that physical and mental support when our men are incarcerated? It's the mothers, grandmothers, wives, sisters, aunts, cousins, and their friends. Women have stood our ground; they have taken on a lot of our roles. Even way back from the 1850s and 1950s until right now it's the women who have stepped up to the plate. Heroic examples include women like Harriet Tubman, Rosa Parks, Angela Davis, Elaine Brown, Patreshia Colors, Angela Rye, and Miracle Boyd, just to name a few. I could fill this entire book up with strong, fearless, unsung women, if it wasn't for these types of women, where would we be? So, let's give them their due respect and stop having this misconception that "women raising a boy to be a man" is not possible, because it is! Peace to my brother Fareed! Thanks again for letting me in on this powerful message about misconceptions!

CHAPTER 14

Fatherhood Part 2 by Mr. Cooley

Fatherhood is a very big and powerful word that we all will experience doing our lifetime in some kind of way. Me, I thank God for review. I say this because I was given the chance to review my life's walk as a father. The truth is, I did not do a very good job. I started out saying to myself, "I'm going to be a better father than my father ever was." But actually, I was worse. I lacked knowledge and understanding, and the bigger thing I lacked in was love, *real* love.

Now let me tell you a little about my story. Coming up as a child, my father was not in our house and times were hard in the 50s (that's the 1950s for you lil' guys). I was the little man of the house and I ran the house like I was the man and father as I got older. I would cook, clean, go out and make money for all eight of us so that the bills would get paid. Yes, my mother was there doing the best she could, but it was too much for one person alone. As time went by, I fell into the model of "by any means necessary". The only understanding I had was to eat and feed my family.

As I got older, life started getting a little better. I ran into a young woman that I truly cared about. A little while later the words came, "We are going to have a baby." I was so happy that I told everyone, "I'm going to be a father." As you can be sure, my street game went up because I needed more money for me, my baby, and my woman "by any means necessary", right? Now there were ten people that I must care for. I'm 20 years old and my child is due July 10, 1976. I want a job but, because I'd been working, I wasn't well educated and with my lack of education, I couldn't get a good job. The jobs I could get would not even pay the bills. This led me deeper into the streets. I was doing well for my family, we eating. My daughter was born. I was still doing me, had $90,000 saved up, a nice apartment with everything in it, a nice neighborhood. I told my guys, "I'm done with the streets now that I am a father." That didn't go down well with them. My guys were broke, because they didn't save a dime. So, they hit me with the guilt trip, how they helped me when I was down. I always knew the saying, "Do me a favor and don't do me no favors!" Yet, under the pressure, I ultimately said, "One more run, but I'm out after this." As fate would have it, not even two months later we got arrested and that got me a 2 to 5-year sentence at Rockview State Penitentiary. My guys (the same guys I sacrificed for) were the ones that told on me. So, because of the selfish decisions I made putting them before my child and woman, I had to fight for my life and freedom back. Being away from my baby, my woman and my family was the hardest thing. Especially being a new father, it was heartbreaking for me.

After my release, I was telling myself: *everything is gonna work out*. I was dealing with my probation officer and just trying to keep the lights and gas on by doing the right things in life. I'm thinking: *Yes, I can go on because with work and a little bit of self-time, I'll be alright.* But that was about me. When did I take the time out for my children? I mean the proper amount of time. These children that were getting older were looking for love and understanding along with so much more that we so-called fathers fail to give.

With this I ask some questions of you:

Fatherhood, what is it to you? What does it mean to be a *real* father? Do you think because your girlfriend said, "Hey, we are having a baby," this makes you a father? The answer is NO! Hearing the announcement, honestly, a lot of us do not know or understand what we have just gotten ourselves into. Why? It's because we weren't even prepared for fatherhood. If your father wasn't there to teach or show you, how could you be prepared? It pains me to say this, yet the truth is always needed to help others in life.

Fast forward to the present. I'm 64 years old, sitting in prison doing "Life" for selling drugs (crack). Eighteen years ago, I was arrested for the final time and they gave me life in jail — no murders, no robbery, no guns, no kidnapping, no home invasions, just drugs.

Some of my children were young, 11, 12, and 13 years old. I gave them everything, or so I thought! I bought them things. What they really wanted and needed was a father. My oldest son almost came to prison with me. I know it was because of me not being a good father. I wish that what I'm about to say will help you in life and in becoming a real father within your house.

Get on the right path. The presence of a man in a child's life is *needed* to guide the child towards his or her own growth and development. A man really helps nurture the qualities needed in a child's life to stimulate their minds towards principle-centered living. The man who takes on the role of a moral educator in a child's life provides guidance and a role model so the child can learn to distinguish the differences between boyhood and manhood. Fatherhood is a state of being, which is actually the foundation that lays down the path towards the future.

A boy is incapable of being a father because he is still trapped in the stage of dependence and immaturity. There's nothing wrong with this stage; it has its place along the path of growth and development. It's a step though, not the end. Only a man is capable of manhood, which is a prerequisite of fatherhood. When a man's on the verge of being a father, he must step on to a new stage of growth and development, the stage at the level of maturity. This enables a man to become capable of independence. Mature independence in turn, allows a father to attain the state of fatherhood by knowing three things: 1) the depth of the responsibilities to our children, 2) being accountable for their well-being and their overall growth and development, and 3) providing, protecting and caring about every aspect of our children's lives.

In conclusion, it must be understood that these are stages of growth that take time to develop with the proper nurturing and guidance. From infant, child, young boy, and teenager, to young man, manhood, and father to fatherhood if these stages are disrupted from the proper flow, most times you end up with the guys seen within the prison walls.

We fathers on the inside are leaving fatherless children out there to draw their own conclusions of what fatherhood is supposed to be about. That, or they'll accept the existing misconception of it. This is one of the main reason's history keeps repeating itself and will continue to do so, until we change our selfish and ignorant ways.

I pray that you are there for your children and, God willing, they will not end up sitting here with me.

CONCLUSION

I just want to thank everyone that read this book or even if you just read bits and pieces of it. Maybe it will be something that you weren't paying attention to or may have missed that will end up helping you or someone you love.

These issues are where a lot of our problems start: having the wrong perception of things and life. Misconceptions!

Again, I must thank everyone that was there for me. You all played a part in me becoming the person I am now, and who I will continue to be. I'm a Muslim man and, in my faith, we recognize that something much greater than me allows us to find balance and pray daily. No matter how much wrong we may do, that balance must be kept in order to assure our good outweighs our bad.

If I forgot to mention anyone, know that it wasn't on purpose. I'm running out of time. This book was supposed to been printed.

I asked my big bro', Cash, a question that made him think. With that he added his thoughts to the book. Thanks again, Bro'. But then he asked me a question that made me think. What is your "net worth"? At the time I really didn't know, but every man should know his net worth, his net worth to his family especially. They may be the ones you have to lead. When I do have my day in court, I won't have to tell them my net worth. I'll be able to show them. Certified paralegal, founder of a non-profit organization, and now an author of a real-to-life self-help and hopefully, motivational book. I didn't give up and I had a plan.

Give me a moment for some of the guys I forgot to mention. Thanks Mr. Cooley, Mal, Sadik, Seek, Reem, Zyhir, Breeze, Giovanni, Deuce, Shy, Fat Boi, Ern, Garfield (Def Jam), my old head Saboor, my old heads Spook and Todd (you help me, I help you; life-time subscriptions), Ameen, Kie, Noon, I almost forgot Rakeeb. I really had the pleasure of meeting some good dudes on my journey. My bro', N.O. said to me, "Through your journey you'll receive justice." *Damn! How right he was.*

To all of you out there, I say: Never give up; always fight. Ya time will come...

ABOUT THE AUTHOR

Fareed Ray is a man that surely has been through his fair share of ups and downs, with the downs out numbering the ups by a lot. His mindset and several misconceptions he chose or grew up to believe caused a lot of his downfalls in life, one of which was a 21-year prison sentence. Then one day Fareed woke up with a very strong desire to right all his wrongs. He also had a strong desire to help others (especially the youth) change the wrong perceptions that 'we as black men and our youth tend to learn all too easily, whether through misguidance or lack of guidance, which starts us off on the road to many failures.

Fareed is also the founder of a non-profit organization MN "Better ways and new ideas save lives." His non-profit organization started off raising money to pay for incarcerated men and women to take correspondence courses to help them make a new path for their future selves. Courses such as paralegal courses, circuit training, as well as college courses were offered. MN has since made plans to expand to also developing learning centers and after school programs for young at-risk adolescents like Fareed was, in hopes of curbing and redirecting their paths in life from wrong to right.

Once Fareed completed his paralegal course, the feeling of accomplishment sparked something in him. That started him out on his new journey in life. The rest is history! If this accomplishment could spark something in him who had already met much defeat and loss, then he knew it could save someone else. Hopefully, he thought, he could touch plenty of African American and other people once they were able to understand our truths and the source of our misguidance.

At the time Fareed Ray started writing this book, he was already incarcerated for more than seven years. He had been denied his first appeal but continued to fight. He wakes up each day doing his best to rectify his affairs and do things to make his mother, children, and wife proud of him.

Now, at the time of this printing, Fareed Ray's second appeal has been granted on the basis of his constitutional rights having been violated. He awaits a court judgement as to whether they will grant him the relief to which the laws say he's entitled. The fight continues. Not just his fight for personal justice, but also to help push his people — us — forward in the race so we don't have to keep coming in last

Place!!!

"I guarantee that these words will spark something in the mind of the person that will add good change for us..." Tupac Shakur [2Pac] (1994, Abbie Kearse Interview, MTV News)

Want to bring your story to life?

Don't have the resources, help or support to do so?
Break Away To Make A Way will Make A Way out od no wat for you..

This book is the first of many to come by CEO of Break Away to Make A Way. Fareed Ray knows first hand about the struggles to Break Away.

Contact Us At:

Fareed Ray
Break Away to Make A Way Publications
PO BOX 61894
Harrisburg, P.A. 17106-1894
Email: Rayfareed@yahoo.com

You don't need any money, just a good story, and I'll take care of the rest. You won't work for me, this will be a partnership!

Made in the USA
Monee, IL
25 September 2021